"Letting her in is...well...dangerous. I can't trust her with my heart and she doesn't trust me with hers. Actually, she doesn't even believe I love her. Of course, I'm not very good at expressing it. I mean, look at me—here at the cabin, far from her."

Randy reached the woods. "I can't risk losing my temper with her."

Years of that very danger flashed through his mind. Of course, their relationship hadn't always been potentially volatile. Jordan's disposition was often sweet. She never used to yell. But these days, she seemed bent on his losing control.

He glanced up at a sky filled with dancing tree limbs. "Please help us, Lord."

Love Letters

by

Annette M. Irby

Robyn,
Thanks for coming in today! All His best in everything.

Annette M. Irby
Zeph. 3:17

This is a work of fiction. Names, characters, places, and incidents are either the product of the author's imagination or are used fictitiously, and any resemblance to actual persons living or dead, business establishments, events, or locales, is entirely coincidental.

Love Letters

COPYRIGHT © 2007 by Annette M. Irby

All rights reserved. No part of this book may be used or reproduced in any manner whatsoever without written permission of the author or The Wild Rose Press except in the case of brief quotations embodied in critical articles or reviews.
Contact Information: info@thewildrosepress.com

Cover Art by *R.J.Morris*

The Wild Rose Press
PO Box 706
Adams Basin, NY 14410-0706
Visit us at www.thewildrosepress.com

Publishing History
First White Rose Edition, January 2007
Print ISBN 1-60154-173-2

Published in the United States of America

Dedication

For the Hero of my life's story, Jesus Christ, whose love letter, the Bible, has changed my life forever.

Chapter One

Randy Ambrose pinned his cell phone against his shoulder and kept typing. Carl must really be agitated to break their "no-calls-on-Sunday" agreement.

"I need that first draft by the twelfth, Randy," his editor reiterated.

"I hear you," Randy answered, absentmindedly. "Thing is, I can't keep writing and focus on a conversation with you at the same time."

"I get it. I get it." Carl's voice sounded agitated. "I'll let you go. Just assure me you can do this?"

Randy stopped typing, reached for his phone and stretched his back. He glanced at the calendar. January 28th, already. "I know you took a chance on me, Carl. I won't blow it. JC Press will like what they see."

"Thanks, I really hope so. We'll be in touch." Carl hung up, freeing Randy to get back to typing. The deadline loomed as he struggled to keep his fingers on the keyboard. If he didn't meet this cut-off date, he'd be facing Carl's wrath and the disdain of the decision makers at

JC Press. They were the first book publisher to give him a chance. He had to impress them. Weariness came over him as he rubbed his temples. He could do this. He had to. His family was counting on him.

****

"Hon!" Jordan called from the living room. "We've got to go."

Randy hit save and glanced at his watch. How had nine a.m. rolled around so quickly? The extra time he tried to give himself every Sunday just swept past him. He closed his laptop. "I'm coming."

Jordan had their twin sons ready to go. She shooed them toward the garage and sent Randy a look. "I don't want to be late."

"I know," he said.

She looked agitated, or he'd offer her a grin. But her usual dimpled smile wasn't in place this morning and her blue eyes lacked their customary sparkle. Her golden brown hair hung over her shoulders in waves, caressing the sweater he'd given her over the holidays. Blue was definitely her color. She pulled a jacket over her slim shoulders.

He refocused. "I was just in the groove."

"Can't you make Sunday morning a priority? Here I am, scrambling to get the kids ready, as well as gather things for my class and you're hibernating."

He tipped his head. "I was writing, Jae. I have a deadline."

"I know." She finished buttoning her coat.

"C'mon, it's not like this happens all the time."

She sighed, reaching into the closet. "I just want Sundays to be reserved for family, that's all. I don't know what's so difficult about that."

Randy thrust his arms into the coat she handed him and took his Bible from her. "Look, I'm doing the best I can. I have to type every chance I get."

She walked ahead of him, opening the hatch of the minivan to put her class supplies inside. "I *know*."

"After the twelfth, things will calm down again," Randy assured. *Then, maybe she'd relax a little.*

Silence wedged its way into the van with them as Randy backed out of the driveway.

"Until the edits come back, anyway," Randy admitted.

"Great. More fun to look forward to."

Randy spent the rest of the drive reworking his latest plot elements in his mind. He glanced at Jordan a couple of times. She faced the window, presumably watching the scenery whiz by.

They rolled into the parking lot of New Walk Church, and Randy held the door as the kids tumbled out. "We're not even late," he noted. Jordan offered no response as she pulled her supplies from the back of the van.

****

Three hours later, Jordan sighed as they entered their split-level home from the garage. She breathed in the warmth of home, thinking how good it would feel to get the gas fireplace going and curl up with something hot to drink. Michigan's nasty winter continued. Last night's low of twelve degrees still held on, leaving the landscape icy. Jordan shivered. For now, she just wanted to get off her feet. Normally, she didn't mind teaching Sunday school. But today, those three-year-olds had worn her out. As she rounded the landing near the front door, she slipped out of her shoes and stepped into her yawning slippers. Her feet pressed into the cushiony softness, soothed. Now, she needed something to comfort her throat.

"What are we having for dinner, Jae?" Randy called as he padded toward her in his wool socks.

"I don't know." She flopped into the easy chair and yanked the handle, sending her into a delicious position for some R&R. With one experienced flick, the throw she'd grabbed on her way down settled over her. The sweater Randy had given her for Christmas was very comfortable, but at this moment, it didn't keep her as warm as she'd like. She shivered under the blanket. He hadn't even mentioned she wore his gift. With his mind so full of that deadline, he probably hadn't even noticed.

"We're starving." He tipped his head and gave her meaningful look. "I've gotta get back to work."

"So make sandwiches; that will take about five minutes. The boys can help." She shifted, trying to get comfortable. "I'm worn out. Cody Markham was absolutely wired today."

"A sandwich? For Sunday dinner?"

So much for the sympathy she had hoped to receive.

"Sure. Why not?"

Jordan didn't have to slide open her lids to know Randy still stood there, green eyes pinned on her, one hand raking through his black hair, another hand perched on his trim waist. He towered over her chair.

"Sandwiches are quick and fuss-free." She tugged the blanket closer to her chin. "Highly recommended."

"Aren't you hungry?"

"Right now, I'm too exhausted to worry about food." She rolled her head away from him. "I'm sorry."

In her mind, she reflected on all the Sunday dinners she'd prepared over the years. This one time she needed a break. Fatigue engulfed her this afternoon. She'd love to help Randy, but she couldn't force herself up right now. Hopefully he understood.

It's difficult to let your guard down when you've just spent three hours hoping one specific troublemaker in the class doesn't pour glue onto anyone else's head. But, with the comfort of her reclining chair and the warmth of the blanket,

Jordan had almost drifted to sleep when banging noises suddenly erupted from the kitchen. She listened for a moment, trying to still her pounding heart, but the noises didn't let up. It sounded as if Randy was pounding frozen foods onto the counter, then tossing them back into the freezer.

She pushed aside the blanket and with effort, stood and stalked into the kitchen on aching feet. "What is the matter, Randy?"

"Don't we have anything to eat?" he bellowed, his head buried in the freezer.

"Sure we do, but you weren't interested in a quick meal." She leaned against the counter for strength. "I thought you had work to do."

Randy slammed the freezer door and pulled his head back to glare at her. "I do. Why can't you just work your magic out here and get dinner going so I can get back to writing?"

"Randy, I'm hurting. I don't feel up to cooking right now. Sandwiches are the best solution." She turned to leave the kitchen. "I'd really appreciate your keeping the noise down."

"Where are you going?"

She turned. "I'm beat. I don't know if you remember this about three-year-olds, but a roomful of them can wear you out. My feet hurt, my back hurts and I'm freezing. I'm going to bed."

"What are we going to do about dinner?"

"Whatever you want."

The boys burst out of their bedroom, having

changed into play clothes. "We're hungry!" they chanted as they ran directly for Jordan.

"Tell Daddy, boys." She pointed them in their father's direction. "I'm going to rest and need all of you to keep it down," she admonished while turning to escape to the master bedroom in search of comfort.

****

Randy tugged the bag of frozen chicken breasts from the freezer and dropped it onto the counter. *Keep it down.* Right. Why couldn't she support his writing? He snagged three pieces from the bag, placed them in a ceramic dish and set the microwave to defrost. Couldn't Jordan see he was doing this for her?

He opened the pantry and found three potatoes for him and the boys. The readout on the beeping microwave told him to flip the meat so it'd thaw evenly. He ignored it for the first two cycles as he scrubbed the potatoes and poked holes in them.

Couldn't Jordan understand he only wanted to take over more of the financial burden in order to take some pressure off her? All he got from her lately was nagging. And today, a perfectly good day for writing, she wouldn't even make them dinner. He yanked open the microwave door and used the tongs to flip the chicken pieces. Only a few more minutes and they would be ready for broiling. Then he could nuke the potatoes.

Where was the seasoning salt? He pulled all

the spices from the cupboard above the stove. Nothing. Maybe she'd hidden the bottle in one of the other cupboards. He opened the nearest door and removed the hot air popcorn popper and the small mixer. Nothing. The next shelf gave up the old coffee maker. Still, no reserved seasoning salt, so he would have to make due with salt and pepper.

He turned the broiler on and pulled out the pan from beneath the stove. Then he laid the chicken breasts out and started the potatoes going in the microwave. The meat only needed a few minutes on each side. Randy was busy throwing a salad together when he smelled a telltale aroma. He pulled open the oven door and sure enough, the chicken was burning. He opened the kitchen window and set the hood fan to high. The fire alarm began blaring throughout the house. He directed the boys to open windows on opposite sides of the upstairs living area, to draw a frigid breeze through. The plan worked and soon the fire alarms went silent. The kids cheered.

Randy felt relief seep through him. It would take a miracle for Jordan to not come out and let him have it. Her disappointment was wearing on him. He longed for a place to write without interruptions. A place like Granddad's cabin. Maybe he would head up there for a few days.

Of course, leaving Jordan to cover everything here wouldn't earn him any points.

However, if he didn't meet this deadline, he may not get another chance with JC Press. His career was on the line along with their financial stability. The freelance work he did couldn't sustain them; they were barely making it on Jordan's salary as an office manager at a local physical therapist's office. Randy longed for the day he could, through writing, cover all their financial obligations. He'd need the royalties from several well-selling books flowing in, along with freelance writing, in order to do it. Then Jordan wouldn't have to work outside the home, and he so longed to give her that freedom. Carl had taken a chance on him, with so few successes under his belt. For Carl's sake and for the family's sake, he had to come through. Maybe he should have settled for sandwiches today, but his mother had always cooked up a feast on Sunday afternoons. So far, Jordan hadn't minded doing that in their married lives. But in reality, it wouldn't have hurt if they'd settled on some ham and Swiss for lunch today. Guilt battered Randy.

Jordan appeared at the doorway to the kitchen in thick socks and a rather unflattering pair of gray sweats. She shielded her eyes. "What is going on?" Her voice sounded like she'd swallowed gravel.

Randy's heart turned over at the sight of her. But irritation prevailed. "Just cooking *dinner*." He stabbed a piece of chicken and sawed off the blackened edges.

The clock chimed one o'clock. "With sandwiches, you would have been typing by now."

Randy cringed. She was right, but anger had snared him. "I can't live on sandwiches."

"Listen, I'm fighting a migraine." She turned. "I'm going back to bed so please try harder to keep it down."

Randy watched her. Part of him ached to make things right, while the other part just wanted her to at least concede he had a valid position.

****

An hour later, Randy stepped through the bedroom doorway. He'd made up his mind. He went into the bathroom for his supplies and returned to the closet to search for his duffel bag.

Jordan peered at him.

"Hi."

"Hi?" She rubbed her temple. "After all that noise, all you can say is hi?"

Randy grimaced. He *had* been loud. "I'll be out of here in a minute."

Randy found his duffel, unzipped it and loaded in the toiletries before snagging open his dresser drawer.

"What are you doing?" Jordan asked, her voice sounding ragged.

Randy threw underwear and socks into the bag, followed by sweatpants and jeans. His favorite sweatshirt lay atop his bureau. He tossed that in as well. "Just getting a couple of things."

Her gaze zeroed in on him.

He peered up at her, bowing over his bag. "I'm going to head to the cabin for a couple of days to try to get some serious work done."

A gust of air from Jordan's lungs elicited a coughing spasm. That didn't bode well, but Randy held to his decision. He'd trade the travel time for a chance at three or so days of uninterrupted writing.

She was already closing down. He'd seen it so many times before—the shuttered expression, the façade of indifference. He watched her tug the blankets under her chin.

"Whatever. Disappear if you want to." She turned away from him. "Say goodbye to the boys."

Randy felt his heart clench. He rezipped his bag and headed for the door. So be it.

Chapter Two

The boys scampered into Jordan's bedroom moments after she heard the gears grinding on the garage door downstairs. She rubbed her head.

"Mommy! Dad left," Aaron announced.

She pushed back the electric blanket and slowly sat up. "I know, sweetie." She swayed a moment, her head dizzy. "Let's go get you both into bed for a nap."

"Aww..." Cassidy and Aaron whined in unison.

"It's Sunday, a restful day," she said, herding them toward the bathroom for a turn apiece. "Okay, now climb into your bunks."

The boys obeyed.

"Behave yourselves. Mommy feels yucky."

The boys didn't cooperate, however, and Jordan spent the next two hours trying to keep them corralled, while fighting a serious headache and the worst sore throat she'd ever had. Finally, she set them up in the rec room with a movie. She bundled up in the living room with the fireplace blazing. Randy could have at least stuck around long enough to supervise the boys so she could rest, couldn't he? Why was he being so selfish? He could have gotten a lot of writing done today, after sandwiches, and monitored the boys through the afternoon.

How she longed for him to be considerate and just maybe take her needs into account sometimes. She worked hard—weekdays outside the home followed by the housework and caring for the boys every evening, sacrificing so he could write. He never seemed to appreciate that. She shivered, wanting so much to get warm. And now, he'd gone off to that cabin! Couldn't he see she needed him here? She could sleep for a week and that'd be just the beginning. She watched the flames dance in the gas fireplace and wished again Randy were there to soothe her needy heart.

****

By the time Randy hit the snow-covered gravel path to his grandfather's cabin, regret had burrowed a deep trough through his heart. He could have at least apologized for being such a maniac about dinner. And what about the kitchen? Jordan hadn't sounded very good when he last saw her. Why hadn't he cleaned it up? She hadn't budged at all, leaving him to cook—mutilate, really—dinner by himself. He sighed again, and caught himself grinding his jaw, more from regret than anger. Jordan probably didn't realize she always pushed him to the limit.

Her indifference was what made him crazy,

made him want to yell. He had to maintain control; though it was especially hard when she closed up and pretended not to care he was leaving for a few days. The real problem was the danger that existed if he ever lost control.

He backed up to the side porch of the cabin and dropped the tailgate on his truck, preparing to offload the supplies he'd bought en route. All these years, he'd kept a key on his ring for this cabin. His breaths came in visible puffs even as he stepped inside. He propped the door open and hauled in two sacks of groceries. Wouldn't be long before he could get to writing.

A familiar stuffy odor lingered and Randy looked around remembering his wife's irritation whenever they'd tried to vacation here. Jordan hated the mustiness and remote location. He recalled her sneezing, complaining and fretting over their twins. Sure, she had allergies and the kids might get a splinter while playing on the old wood floors. But if she'd just try, she might find this place full of potential and character. His grandfather had built this cabin forty years ago. It was the perfect place to visit when Randy's life was messy. If Granddad were here, he'd brew coffee and stoke up the fire, then invite Randy to play Scrabble so they could chat between turns about his life and problems.

Randy threw his duffel bag toward the old sofa and watched a cloud of dust plume. Glad he didn't have to anticipate Jordan's response, he continued settling in. After wasting most of the day, the itch to write was overwhelming. But the essentials had to be in place first.

He left snowy boots near the door and shivered. Thankfully, there were still dry chunks of wood by the fireplace. He rifled through a kitchen drawer to find some matches. After using decade-old newspapers from beside the woodbin as kindling and opening the flue, he got a fire going. He stood, already feeling its warmth. The scent of burning wood soon overpowered the aromas of must and sulfur from the match.

The generator he'd fired up outside would supply power for the lights, the fridge and the heaters, but a fire in the fireplace was closer to how Granddad used to do things. Sure, Randy would turn on the wall heaters, but he wouldn't rely on them alone until bedtime when he couldn't monitor a fire. Right now, the cabin felt like a freezer. Randy walked around clicking on strategically located heaters—in the bathroom, the kitchen and dining room. The hot smell of unused heaters heating up made him revisit each one of them after a few minutes just to be sure they were working properly.

Several minutes later, feeling a bit thawed, he donned his boots and coat once more for a trip to the woodpile beside the cabin. He'd bring in several more pieces for drying, though he wasn't sure how long he'd be staying. Outside the air smelled thickly of wood smoke from his chimney, but the wind was picking up to scour the air.

A forecasted blizzard would zero in on him tonight. So be it. He could write nearly anywhere. The generator would provide power, and he had heat either way. The inspiration of writing here, surrounded by reminders of Granddad, would help him focus.

Randy turned toward the kitchenette to make coffee, shoving thoughts of Jordan away. She likely had the boys in bed by now and was enjoying a cup of tea and watching an old movie. He wanted to settle on that mental image, but the sound of her voice when she'd spoken before he left kept haunting him—such a raspy sound.

Oh, Jordan...

Randy poured coffee over the lump in his throat. Here, alone, his self-protection mechanisms weren't necessary. But even now, he wouldn't let down his guard. If he shattered here, who would collect the pieces?

Randy set the bag holding his laptop on the table. The chirping electronic beeps as his computer booted up sounded out of place here in this rustic setting. But Randy's novel was set here, so he didn't mind. He spread his outline beside his computer and found the pencil line marking his place. As the wind picked up outside, he pushed his hand through his black hair and read over the last few paragraphs.

Chapter Three

Jordan awoke sweating. Fatigue lingered, as did the threat of a headache. She had to avoid tension tonight, or she'd be battling a nasty migraine by midnight. Swallowing, she tested her throat and had to squeeze her eyes shut at the raw resistance. She padded to the kitchen to heat the teakettle, hoping to hydrate herself before lack of water contributed to her symptoms.

She staggered to a halt at the sight of the kitchen. Every small appliance they owned lay on the counters, and the sink was piled high with dirty dishes. Randy had even pulled appliances out he couldn't have possibly used this afternoon—the mixer for one. Even the old hot air popper lay tilted on the counter. The broiler pan, encrusted with burned grease, lacked the tinfoil that would have made clean-up much easier. Jordan wanted to cry. This proved it again. Randy didn't care. If he truly loved her, he wouldn't have left such a mess for her to clean up. If he loved her, he wouldn't have abandoned her to carry the entire family burden, while she was feeling awful.

She flicked off the stove when the kettle whistled and made herself focus on righting the kitchen. The boys appeared for a snack, but she put them off. "You need to clean up after lunch, you two."

"But Daddy said not to this time, Mom," Aaron said, his eyes wide. He'd trusted that by obeying Randy he wouldn't be disobedient to his mother. Jordan felt her heart squeeze.

"It's okay, kiddo." She smoothed her palm over his face. "No worries. Let's just get this cleaned up, okay? Bring the dishes from that counter over to the sink, and I'll load the dishwasher."

An hour later the kitchen still wasn't perfect, but the bulk of the mess had been straightened. Jordan barely dragged herself to the recliner in the living room, a cup of tea in her hands. The boys inhaled granola bars and glasses of milk before heading down to the rec room once more.

Blueberry tea released a heady fragrance into the room, and Jordan wrapped her hands around the mug. She reached into the pocket of the chair and drew out the novel she was currently reading. Christian fiction, with a good dose of romance, should help her lose herself. Randy had evidently lost himself. No doubt he was happily ensconced at his granddad's old cabin, writing away. Glad to be free of her. And unless he had brought his cell phone re-charger, after a day or so there was no way she could reach him. That rustic place didn't have a landline or good cell phone reception; it barely had running water.

Near dinnertime, Jordan fed the boys grilled cheese and got them into bed. They had school tomorrow. A bit of extra sleep tonight would do them good, and it would give her some time to herself.

She boiled water in a saucepan for oatmeal to soothe her throat and reheated the teakettle. The wind picked up, spooking her. With the boys in bed, she could do anything she wanted, maybe read in bed with the lights blazing or take a long, leisurely bath. Anything. But…nothing appealed to her. The wind whistled past the house. She dreaded the possibility of trees coming down on them or branches crashing through windows.

Fear kept her from going for a peek into the darkness to discern the flailing limbs of bare trees. She'd feel a whole lot safer if Randy were home tonight.

She sat by the fireplace, swiveling her chair to face the flames. So far, the chills and fever hadn't returned. Maybe that bout with whatever it was had passed.

"Lord, I think I pushed him away again," she prayed. "I don't know why that always seems to happen. Please bring him home." She paused a moment, feeling the heat radiating toward her. "And give me the grace to apologize, hear him out and…oh, help us relate differently.

I don't know what's wrong. But it's wearing me out."

She sat there a long time, staring into the flames. Around nine-thirty, she meandered back to their cold, empty bedroom, wishing again Randy were home. She clicked on the electric blanket and washed up before climbing into bed, still worried about the wind.

****

He had intended to write, but the sound of snow pelting the window stirred something in Randy. He donned his boots and coat and stepped out onto the porch. There he stood witnessing the wind's power in the gigantic spruce trees. The branches stirred, twisting, but giving in to the forces. Even the darkness couldn't blot out their majesty. Randy wanted to ride the branches, sixty feet in the air, at the mercy of the storm. But his days of adventure had faded with the responsibilities of marriage and family. He'd climbed a couple of spruces as a child which nearly gave his grandfather a heart attack the first time he found him up there. That high, his father couldn't reach him. No one could, except God. The only harm, a windstorm. Or lightning.

The air felt sucked from the porch. Then a mighty gust tore through, stealing away Randy's breath. He could almost predict the wind, but there had been no predicting his father. All he'd had at home was fear. Out here, he could ride his fears out, battle them, though invisible they remained.

Jordan reminded him of wind. She could become furious, stirring him up. But he'd learned to wait her out. What he couldn't do was let his own storm loose. That kind of squall he couldn't predict.

And no matter what he did or said, she held something of herself back from him, some piece of her heart.

He wished she were the only one doing that.

Randy stepped off the porch. The wind ripped his breath away. He thrust his hands into his pockets, but raised his chin, waiting it out.

Aiming himself toward the woods behind the cabin, he stepped off.

The spruces stood between the cabin and the woods. Out there, the effects of the storm would surround him. If a branch tore away, or a tree toppled, he'd be right there.

"Jesus, my marriage is a mess. I can't let her in, though. So, if that's what You're going to say, sorry." He looked up to the top of a tilting white pine. "Letting her in is...well...dangerous. I can't trust her with my heart and she doesn't trust me with hers. Actually, she doesn't even believe I love her. Of course, I'm not very good at expressing it. I mean, look at me—here at the cabin, far from her."

Randy reached the woods. "I can't risk losing my temper with her."

Years of that very danger flashed through

his mind. Of course, their relationship hadn't always been potentially volatile. Jordan's disposition was often sweet. She never used to yell. But these days, she seemed bent on his losing control.

He glanced up at a sky filled with dancing tree limbs. "Please help us, Lord."

Randy could make out very little this far from the porch light. Snow blew all around him; sculpting drifts and obscuring the landscape, hiding the cabin that surely stood somewhere back there. He tucked his head down and burrowed into the wind. If he walked straight back in this direction, he'd find it. No fictional episode of getting lost in the storm for him.

With steady paces, Randy retraced his steps. He'd seen anger. He'd seen rage. He wouldn't be responsible for letting his anger go, buttons pushed, or not. His father had been like a grizzly when he'd gotten riled, but Granddad's cabin had always been his refuge. Now, when Jordan pushed him toward the edge, Randy retreated. It wasn't wimpy. It was wise. At least that is what he'd always told himself. While he usually stayed home with her, so they could make up hours later, tonight he couldn't even call her. His cell phone wouldn't get service this deep into no-man's-land.

Yes. He'd seen what anger and rage could do. His own body bore rage's bragging rights. He knew his mother's had too. In fact, his mother's death had been rather mysterious to then nine-year-old Randy. One thing he'd learned was that you just don't ask too many questions.

Of course, anger or not, he wouldn't put himself in the same club with his father. For one, Randy's dad had never given his life to Jesus. But Granddad had seen to it that Randy understood his need for a Savior at an early age. Randy's mind slipped back to one of his stays here at the cabin. Near the creek the summer he turned eight, Granddad had shared the mystery of God's forgiveness.

Randy tugged on his fishing line. "Tell me again, Granddad."

Durham settled back against the tree on the shore. "Well, it's like this. God didn't want to be without you, Randy. But you've sinned in your life, so He made a way for you to be forgiven. Like a loving father, He suffered for you."

"A loving father?" Randy recalled the bitterness and question in his heart even then. He hadn't had that example.

"Yes. See, your earthly dad isn't perfect. But Jesus is. He came to earth as a baby and then He grew up. And all that while, guess what?"

"What?"

"He never sinned." Granddad stretched his legs in front of him. "That meant he could die for you and me, in our place."

"I don't want to die."

"I know. But, because of your sins—lying, being mean or disobedient—you deserve to die."

"Wow." Randy couldn't have been more

impressed. "And God took that punishment for me?"

"On His own body. The soldiers were very cruel to Him. And although He knew what was coming, He went through it anyway because of something very important. Do you know what that was?"

Randy shook his head, completely hooked.

"Love."

"I know about that."

Granddad ruffled his hair. "You do, huh?"

"Yeah, it's what I feel for my dog." Randy referred to his grandfather's German shepherd mix, a dog he only saw when he visited.

"He's mine, my boy, but I know what you mean."

Randy reached over to pet the sleeping animal and think through everything his grandfather had shared, though he'd heard it all before. The ideas baffled him, but he couldn't resist the message. "Okay, tell me again what I need to do."

Granddad drew a deep breath. "You take His sacrifice seriously."

For the first time, Randy turned to fully face his grandfather. He handed over his fishing line and said, "That's exactly what I want to do. Take it seriously."

Durham settled the pole in his hands, automatically wiggling the line every now and then. "Okay, then you pray to God and tell Him that."

"Simple as that?"

"Yup." Tears filled Granddad's eyes while Randy knelt there on the creek's grassy bank and offered a prayer to God. "Lord, I wanna take Your love and sacrifice very seriously. I do. Granddad once told me You wanna live inside of me. Okay, do that. And thanks for forgiveness. I need that. Okay. Amen." Randy looked up. "Like that?"

"Sure, little guy." He reached a gnarled hand over and rubbed Randy's head. "Just like that."

The memory faded, and Randy swallowed against the lump in his throat. He wondered again if he had truly employed forgiveness in his own life, where his father was concerned. He had to wonder, since anger was such a threat to him. Rage didn't plague him. He'd been tamed, at least at some level, by God's love and fathering. But he still held bitterness toward his dad.

Randy reached the cabin and decided to circle it.

His father had died when he was seventeen. As a litmus test to see if he'd forgiven him, he examined his heart. Nope, he still felt relief and a bit of something he'd rather not name. Elation? He cringed. It looked like this thing still had a hold of him. Standing here as the wind bit into his face, he ground out some choice words about his life, his wife and his plight. He came around to the porch once more. Fisting his hands inside thick gloves, he tromped up the stairs and kicked snow from his boots. When he was inside, he peeled off his sweaty pullover and tugged a fresh one from his bag, along with dry wool socks. Then, he turned toward the woodstove.

Fisting his hands once more, he took a deep breath, knowing God was asking something of him in the quiet of this place. He knelt on the ancient rug. "Okay, Lord, I want to forgive my dad. I don't want to be held captive by his actions any longer, always worried about losing my temper. I know I'm not the person I once was. I want to fully be the person You want me to be. Help me forgive my dad. Help me let it all go. I bring it to the cross and I leave…" his voice cracked. He swallowed a few times, fighting the tears that wouldn't be stemmed. One slipped from each eye. He brushed them away, though no one watched except God. "I lay all the pain at the foot of Your cross. And I will leave it there."

There was no way of knowing if that moment had truly freed him from the past. Only time would tell. And in the meantime, Randy still couldn't risk too much. His earlier years had proven his temper. He didn't ever want Jordan to see that.

Randy pulled a notepad from the stack of materials on the table and snatched a pen as he headed toward the sofa. The only way to unblock his writing was to get out what needed to be said.

Chapter Four

Jordan hustled Cassidy and Aaron out the door to school Monday morning. She'd have to watch them from the house. Her throat felt skinned this morning and her temperature was hovering around 101°F. She pulled her robe tighter. She ached all over and getting the boys ready for school had been a chore.

The twins were out of sight for several yards of their journey to the bus stop, but she caught glimpses of them between the houses and trees. The bus crept past on the crunching snow and a minute later, she waved at what she thought were her sons as the bus headed down the hill toward the school.

She'd called into the physical therapist's office at seven so they could find coverage. Perhaps Amy could work today. If all else failed, the answering service could catch the phones.

She sighed and headed to the kitchen for hot tea with lemon and honey. Toast was out of the question. Perhaps oatmeal would work, again. Later.

Once more, she longed for Randy to be home with her. His days were usually spent holed up in his office clicking away on his keyboard, pounding out a story or article. If she was going to be on sick leave, she'd prefer Randy's company to the lonely house.

Tea in hand, she headed to the sofa. She'd need a blanket and pillow from her bed. The thought of dragging those items back in here seemed tiring. Why bother? She kept walking past the sofa, straight to her room. A couple more hours of sleep would do her good. She sipped half her cup of blended tea and couldn't keep her eyes open. Lying down, she drifted off to sleep.

Half an hour later, the phone rang. Her office's number came up on the caller ID. Why would they be calling? Since she could barely whisper, even calling in sick this morning had been challenging. She let the call go to voicemail. That way, she could listen in a few moments, without being expected to speak. If it was urgent, she'd call them back; if not, she'd sleep.

Amy left a message saying she could fill in this entire week if Jordan needed her beyond today. She wished Jordan well and hung up. Glad for the friendly message, Jordan tried to relax again. She swallowed some now-cool tea, her throat aching, and curled onto her side.

If the boys weren't at school, with the possibility of an emergency coming up there, she'd have turned the ringer off, especially after it rang five times forty-five minutes later and then immediately began ringing again. She was going to ignore it and let whoever it was talk to voicemail. If the school wanted her they would try her cell phone second. She had that nearby. The next call urged her across the bed to at least check the display on the phone she'd left on her husband's nightstand. Maybe it'd be Randy.

****

That same morning in the cabin, Randy awoke sore. He sat and rolled his neck, then his shoulders. So much for that night's sleep. A hot shower helped, but painkillers would do more. He sorted through his bags and found none. Then he searched drawers and cabinets. A bottle of aspirin that expired in 1986 rested on the shelf. Not great, but it would have to do. His stomach growled, so he began putting together an omelet with the ham, eggs, cheese and green pepper he'd brought with him. The coffee's scent danced with his breakfast's as he cooked. His head still ached with neck pain and now he could add caffeine withdrawal. In his hurry at the grocery store he'd grabbed decaf, not his first choice.

After breakfast, Randy couldn't settle down to type. He paced instead. It was time to think through his options. He'd been here about fifteen hours, survived a mild blizzard, pined for Jordan and missed his boys. But he hadn't been writing.

Randy stood at the window, watching the

snow fall. What if Jordan decided to pull the kids out of school early and drive out here to see him? He was only fifty miles from home. A long drive in this weather, but not too bad. Maybe they would patch things up and head home even tonight, together.

****

After the call turned out to be a wrong number, Jordan gave up trying to sleep. Her high temperature had broken again but her throat felt shredded. She tried to keep up with fluids, even though they seemed to scrape going down. She'd even resorted to taking liquid children's Tylenol, which seemed to be helping.

She tugged on her robe and meandered to the kitchen for something smooth to eat. After downing a banana, she decided to read before remembering she had just finished the last of the stack of novels she had borrowed from the local library. She wandered into the rec room. Nothing on the bookshelf interested her. Maybe Randy had some interesting reading in his office. He often purchased novels to keep his own inspiration moving forward. He'd told her reading other people's fiction made him want to write his own.

She scanned the shelves. Nothing they hadn't discussed or that she hadn't already read. Her eyes moved to the closet. The door was open. Though she was never one to investigate his messy piles, she found herself drawn somehow.

Her gaze landed on the askew cover of one box. She lifted the cover and under a square piece of cardboard, she found piles of letter-sized envelopes. She couldn't tell by the paper just how old they were. On the shelf under Randy's printer he kept vellum paper, a special effect making it look fashionably aged. These letters reminded her of that paper. But, who were they to? She pulled an envelope from the stack and sank into his office chair.

Before she opened the envelope, her fuzzy mind drifted over the possibilities. She didn't make it a practice to invade his privacy but he wasn't here to ask. She could try his cell, but with her whispery voice, he might hang up on her, if she even got through. The letters might not even be his. What if they were letters from a past girlfriend, or worse yet, *to* a past love? Curiosity grappled with her conscience. What could it hurt to read just one of them? If they were to a past fling, from before they met, she'd just put it back and ask him later why he kept them. If they were from him to someone else, she'd ask why he never wrote letters to her. It was easier to believe they were to him. Whoever it was, he or she had been prolific. The stacks of envelopes in the box were quite a testimony. Overpowering all tentacles of guilt, Jordan unfolded the vellum-like paper and began reading.

Chapter Five

Randy set aside his notebook. He finally felt focused enough to work on his novel.

By two p.m., hunger pains in his stomach were too intense to ignore. At least, he'd gotten two full chapters in. If only he could always be that productive.

He threw together a ham sandwich and sat down to read what he'd written. Most of it was salvageable. The morning's success brought a grin to his face. He could do this. He almost wanted to call Carl and celebrate. However, he still had several chapters to write before this story was even in first draft state and then he'd have to rework it. The last days of January were upon him and the twelfth of February crept ever closer. If things weren't so tense with his wife, he'd probably be further by now. Overwhelmed by the sheer volume of work he had left to do, Randy's fingers itched to get back to it.

But, after gulping down the sandwich, Randy's thoughts couldn't settle on the story once more. They kept drifting to Jordan. He took up a pen and drew his notebook closer.

Love Letters

J,
I could never tell you this in person.

****

Jordan scanned to the bottom of the page. It was signed: *With all my love, R.* She worried a nail. Randy?

The kids would be home in twenty minutes. She should meet them at the bus stop at the end of the block. Her groan sounded strained as she let her eyes settle back on the letter. Maybe she had time to read it before changing from her pajamas and robe.

****

Randy penned neat, quick strokes on the page, pouring out his heart to his wife, though she'd never see it. He'd written three-and-a-half pages, when he stopped and scanned the latest paragraph.

...if only you'd believe me. I've never met anyone like you. We match up like God always intended us to meet. Didn't He? But you won't believe I love you. What should I do? Words haven't worked, and gifts can't express it. How can I get through? So many years of the same challenge. Oh, I love you. But what good are my words, if you don't, can't, receive them?

Randy gulped against the recurring swelling in his throat. *Aww, Jae...* He squeezed his eyes shut and swallowed again.

Then he knew what he had to do. Yes, just

exactly how to prove his love.

****

I know we only just met. But spending Sundays at the lake and heading to Mackinac Island...I love being with you, hearing your voice, seeing your smile. I love your shining auburn hair, blue eyes and dimples. Aww, J... How could I tell you? You're adorable. You're priceless and wherever this is headed, you'll always be special, the most precious of all.

How I hope you'll let me be a part of your future.

She considered her hair more golden brown than reddish. But perhaps ten years ago, that's how he'd seen her. As far as dimples were concerned, they weren't very pronounced. He must have really studied her face, even back then.

She reread some of the phrases and caught her breath. He'd never said things like these in person. Why not? What was it that silenced him? She glanced at the open closet door.

She wondered if Randy would be home that evening. How many letters did she dare read before he returned?

The sound of the boys tromping up the wooden front steps brought Jordan quickly out of her chair. Too quickly, in fact. She dropped back into the chair to breathe through the wooziness swamping her congested head.

The doorbell rang moments later as she

tried again. Two little faces appeared at the slim windows as she rounded the corner from Randy's office. The twins wore a bit of concern on their wind-kissed faces. She smiled up at them and took the half staircase to the front door.

The boys brought snow and mud inside with them. They chattered excitedly about special goings on at school for Valentine's Day but Jordan couldn't focus very well. She shivered, standing there on the tile, glad they'd gotten fully inside so she could close out the cold.

"Hey, Mom! We did it. We walked home from the bus stop all by ourselves."

"Good job, boys," she said, trying her voice.

"Are you still feelin' sick, Mommy?" Cassidy asked, a sweet look of concern in his eyes.

She hugged him. "I think I'm feeling better, kiddo. Thanks." Such a precious gift, these boys.

"Let's get you two a snack. I bet you're hungry."

"Starving!" Aaron hollered, pounding up the stairs in stocking feet.

She sliced up an apple and chopped off a few chunks of cheese per twin and went to sit in the recliner. May as well stamp the rest of the afternoon and evening with the phrase: *endurance required.*

****

Darkness descended early with snow flurries ticking against the cabin's windows. Tomorrow morning, Randy would put his plan into action. In the meantime, perhaps he could access that place of productivity once more.

****

At eight-fifteen, Jordan finally settled down with hot tea. First, she'd take her temperature. Chills had grabbed hold of her again this evening. Her throat still felt raw and a sinus headache lingered. She'd fed the boys scrambled eggs with ham for dinner. Soup was all she could handle for herself. Now, the boys were in bed and would doubtless drift off soon. The thermometer beeped and she tugged it free. The numbers confirmed a fever of 101.5. Just great. She was getting worse. She'd probably better see her doctor tomorrow. Thoughts of going out when she felt this miserable made her burrow deeper beneath the afghan she'd spread over herself.

Here was her chance, fever and all, to read more of those letters. She pulled one from the stack she'd carried upstairs from Randy's office.

Her conscience niggled again. But she squelched the concern with the thought that the letters were obviously to her, so why shouldn't she read them?

She sipped her honey and lemon-laced tea and began to read.

Sweet J,
Now that we've been married a little over a month, I have to get my thoughts down on paper. I had no idea it would be this wonderful.

Watching you sleep, hearing you sing in the shower, loving you...I've tried telling you, but I'm not sure I'm getting it right. For some reason, I can't seem to say how much I love you out loud. And whenever I try, it seems...well, it's not a place we linger. Why is that? I do love you, J. More than I ever thought possible.

With all my love, R

Jordan lifted her gaze to the gas fireplace and absently watched the flames dance against the fireproof "log." Oh, the heat.

These love letters made sense. They allowed Randy to get his thoughts down on paper. Unfortunately, he had always preferred writing to spending time with her.

She reached for the bottle of children's acetaminophen for a dose and discovered it nearly empty. Hopefully the boys wouldn't come down with what she had. They couldn't swallow pills yet and with her throat, she didn't want to. Some medicine should kick this fever and ease the pain.

She closed her eyes, swallowing the last of the cherry-flavored syrup. It stung going down but it was a small price to pay.

Her mind again drifted to Randy, and she let herself extend some grace toward him. These letters were getting to her. The contrast of yesterday's strain with today's love notes was stark. Indeed, the contrast of Randy in person and the Randy of these letters was unsettling.

Did her writer husband truly find it so difficult to express his feelings to her?

Getting honest with herself, Jordan wondered how she'd respond if Randy began relating these sentiments to her in person. Honestly? She'd probably quickly change the subject.

Her fuzzy mind didn't follow the thoughts any further, preferring to fault Randy rather than question her own responsibility.

She decided to call in to the office tonight and let them know her condition. She left a raspy message, glad Amy could cover all week if needed. Right now, she couldn't imagine feeling well enough to go to work for at least the next two days. Plus, the office's policy stated there had to be a twenty-four hour window following a fever before returning to work. She couldn't boast that kind of track record over the last day and a half.

Clicking off the phone, her thoughts returned to Randy. They'd fallen in love while in college. She appreciated his warmth and kindness. He stood a few inches taller than her, with long bangs that fell in his eyes those early days. She loved his green eyes and his strength. All these thoughts of him made her wish him home. Maybe he would pack up and simply appear. Any minute now she'd hear the garage door begin grinding away on its gears under the boys' room. Why not call him and make the first move? Scooping up the phone, she dialed his cell phone and waited.

****

Randy heard his phone chirp and pulled it from his belt clip in amazement. He hadn't seen any sign of service on the screen since he'd gotten here. But the readout displayed: Home. He pressed the button to answer the call.

****

"Randy?" Jordan rasped.

All she heard was the faint sound of Randy saying, "Hello...? Hello?"

"Randy, it's me. Can you hear me?"

"Jordan?"

"Hi," she said, relieved to have gotten through.

"I can barely hear you, honey. Speak up."

"I can't. I'm sick."

"Sick? Oh, man."

"I need you," she confessed.

She heard shuffling on his end.

"What?" he asked.

"Please, can you just come home?"

"I'm sorry, Jordan. I'm moving all over the cabin to try to hear you better. The service is very bad up here. Say that again."

"I need you to come home," she rasped, tears stinging her eyes as her throat protested.

"I'm sorry, Jordan. I know we're still connected, but I can't make out your words anymore. Listen, if you can still hear me, I'm sorry about yesterday. I-I miss you...a lot. I can't stop thinking about you. I...love—"

The line beeped three successive times indicating they'd been disconnected. Jordan glanced at the screen as it returned to default mode. A lump crowded into her prickly throat.

"Oh, Randy," she whispered. "Why are you so far away when I need you?" A sob settled into her chest, but Jordan swallowed against it. At least he had understood she was sick and she'd gotten to hear his voice. Her gaze fell to his letters. Crying made her throat and head ache more, so she'd try to mine comfort from the letters. She raised the lever on the side of the chair, stood and carried the priceless correspondence back to the master bedroom. She quickly burrowed under the covers, not caring she was dressed in sweats. If she read until she fell asleep, at least it would seem like Randy cared. Obviously, if he really did care, he'd be here holding her tonight.

****

Randy ground out a few unwholesome words between clenched teeth when he realized his phone had dropped her call. There she was, right there on the line. But at least he'd been able to tell her he loved her. Hopefully she'd heard him.

First light, nothing. He'd put his plan into action tonight.

Chapter Six

Jordan stirred as Randy stepped into their room. The hall light had probably awakened her. He quickly moved back and flipped off the wall switch. During the last two hours on the road, all he could think about was her voice, so raspy and raw. He padded around the room as quietly as possible.

After pausing a few moments for his eyes to adjust to the darkness, he deposited his duffel bag in front of the closet door, out of the path to the bed. He sat on the chair in the corner and tugged off his socks and sweatshirt, and then made his way toward the bathroom where he took care of a few necessities. The nightlight in the bathroom helped him make out where everything was. His pajamas hung from the hook on the door and he donned them quickly. Finishing in there, he quietly pulled open the bathroom door and started toward the bed.

Bam! He kicked a foot rail on the bed and bit his knuckle to keep from howling.

"Aaron? Cassidy?" Jordan rasped.

"Sorry," Randy whispered, his heart pounding. The last thing he wanted to do right now was rob her of more rest.

"Go to bed, boys. Mommy's still feeling sick," she mumbled, rolling over on her side. "You're okay. Just go back to bed."

"Okay," Randy murmured without moving, waiting for her to fall asleep again. When she was still for several moments, her ragged breathing evened out and Randy felt safe to continue toward his side of the room. His fingers grazed the comforter as he felt his way along the foot of the bed, though he was careful not to touch Jordan. His toe still throbbed as he peeled back the covers and rested his weight on the other foot.

Now, the trick was to get into bed without her noticing.

Jordan didn't stir again, even when her alarm clock blasted regular spurts of aggravation at seven a.m. Randy reached across her and silenced it. Hovering over her, he noticed how hot she felt. Why hadn't he thought to check her temperature earlier? The backs of his fingers pressed against her forehead. She was burning up. He went in search of the thermometer, leaving the closet light on and the door nearly closed. On his way by, he woke the boys. They cheered when they saw him, but he grinned and shushed them while offering hugs.

"I'm going to help you get ready this morning, but I need you to do as much as you can without me. Get dressed and try to start breakfast. I'll be out in a minute and please, boys, stay quiet," Randy admonished and ducked into the master bedroom with the thermometer at the ready. He'd had to resort to the mercury-filled kind since he couldn't find the digital one.

Jordan moaned when he positioned it under her arm. Thankfully, her collar allowed him access. He watched to be sure she didn't move her arm. Three minutes felt like an eternity when he couldn't move.

The sun hadn't yet risen this morning, so the room was pocketed in shadows. In the low light, he could make out the shapes around the room including several envelopes beside the bed and piled on the nightstand. Randy picked up an unfolded letter and recognized it right away. Had she been reading this whole stack? One of the letters even rested between their pillows. What did she think of these?

He glanced at her sleeping face, glad he'd followed his instinct and returned the previous night. He couldn't imagine Jordan getting up to help prepare the boys for school when she wasn't even lucid enough to recognize he'd come home, to hear the alarm or even awaken when he touched her. Four minutes had passed by the time he pulled the thermometer out to read it. One hundred and three. *Oh, boy.*

He went for some water and ibuprofen caplets in the kitchen. In the meantime, Cassidy was trying to spread toast with peanut butter. It appeared that Aaron had attempted to pour milk from the two-thirds full gallon jug and managed to slosh about as much into the bowl as beside it.

"It's all right, Aaron, just wipe it up and eat your cereal." Randy offered an encouraging smile to his son. "You guys are doing great."

"Where's mommy?" Cassidy asked.

"Asleep. She's got a fever and she hurts really bad."

"Oh," Aaron said around a mouthful of cereal. "Poor mommy."

"So, let's stay very quiet, okay?" The boys nodded. "Good. I'll be back in a few minutes. Fill up your tummies."

Their boys, whose metabolisms matched that of racehorses, could eat hearty breakfasts, lunches and dinners; yet remain on the thin side of average. He and Jordan had to stay diligent about getting them to eat enough.

Randy found the medicine and carried a glass of water with the pills back to the bedroom. He flipped on the light in the bathroom. Jordan still hadn't stirred.

"Honey?" Randy set the drink and pills on the nightstand. "Jae?"

Her eyes began to flutter open. He watched her try to focus.

"Surprise. I'm home," he murmured, grinning.

She opened her mouth, but the scratching sound her vocal chords made prompted Randy to say, "Don't try to talk." He brushed the hair back from her forehead. "I'm sorry for everything. I'm going to take care of you today. The boys are getting ready for school. You can rest without worrying about anything."

Tears came to her eyes and she closed them. He brushed the drops away with his thumbs before they could run down to the pillowcase. "Listen, Jae. You have a fever and need to take some IB. Okay?"

She nodded without speaking.

"Can you sit up?"

She tried, but moaned, probably aching from head to toe. The sound wrenched his heart. "Let me help you." He lifted her gently, supporting her back until she was upright and then holding her there while offering her the pills with his free hand. When she'd placed them on her tongue, he handed her the water.

After she'd swallowed, Randy encouraged her to drink some more water. She did, but then wanted to lie down.

"Go back to sleep. I'll check on you after I get the boys on the bus."

She nodded as he tucked her in.

****

After walking the boys to the bus stop, he cleared a path to the door and came in to call their family doctor. If this thing had been hanging on since Sunday and had only gotten worse, she probably needed antibiotics. Soon, he wanted to discuss the letters on their bedroom floor. But right now, Jordan's health was his number one concern.

The doctor could see them in an hour. Randy entered the bedroom to find the bed empty. Jordan appeared from the bathroom, wrapped in a bathrobe.

The letters were nowhere in sight.

"Jae, I made an appointment with Dr. Benson. He'll see us in an hour. Do you want help getting ready?"

She looked at him. How he wished she could talk. Was that surprise in her eyes? She studied him.

"What?"

She shook her head, touching her throat.

"Let's get you bundled up. Still feeling feverish?" He put the back of his hand on her forehead and slipped a palm down her cheek. "You're a lot cooler."

She nodded and sat on the bed.

Randy pulled jeans and a thick turtleneck sweater from her dresser, but Jordan insisted on taking over from there.

"I'm going to go make tea and oatmeal. It's only ten minutes to the clinic. We have time for breakfast."

Jordan stepped into the bathroom with her clothes and Randy searched the room for any sign of the letters. He didn't find them in her nightstand or under the bed. Her dresser drawers squeaked when he tried to open them so he stopped. She'd hidden them. What good was her discovery of the letters if she didn't even want him to know she'd found them?

This wasn't exactly how he'd planned things.

His cell phone chirped as he boiled water in the kitchen. Carl. Randy didn't want to answer, but duty won out. "Hey, Carl."

"How are you doing, Randy?"

"Okay."

"Got a first draft done yet?"

"Not quite." Several chapters short of that milestone, actually.

"It's the first, Randy," Carl said, stating the date.

"I know. My wife is sick with a nasty fever. We're on our way to the clinic. I'll be writing this afternoon, though."

Carl was silent, no doubt worrying. Randy offered, "If I have to miss sleep until the twelfth, I *will* email you a completed manuscript in at least second draft form. On time."

"Polished would be better."

"I know." Randy rubbed his whiskers. He hadn't shaved in three days. Perhaps he could fit that in before their drive to the doctor's office. "Listen, I gotta go. We're on a tight schedule this morning."

"Randy, I'm sorry your wife is sick. But, we can't do this *for* you. Don't let us down."

"I won't."

Randy beeped off his phone and measured oatmeal for two servings. Then he brought orange juice and a banana to the table. When the teakettle shrieked, he turned off the gas and poured Jordan a mug of tea. The spicy fragrances of apple and cinnamon rose with the steam toward his nose.

She appeared and settled at the table, looking at him. Her pensive gaze and inability to talk was likely to make him crazy. "Do you want to try milk this morning, too?"

She held up her thumb and index finger, about an inch apart, indicating *a little*. She dropped raisins into her hot cereal and he set them swimming in the milk he poured on. They ate a quiet meal together with Randy mentally writing his story and Jordan's eyes on him.

****

The doctor ordered a swab of Jordan's throat that he said would take a day to process. In the meantime, since he was fairly certain she suffered from strep throat, he prescribed antibiotics. He cautioned her, however, that if the test results came back negative the clinic would call her and she could quit taking the medication. They filled the prescription at the pharmacy on the way out and Randy helped Jordan back into the car. Of course, she hadn't spoken much all morning. That, combined with the way she kept studying him, had changed their entire dynamic. Randy focused on being attentive but struggled as plotlines scurried through his mind.

At home, Jordan indicated with flat palms pressed together and brought to her cheek that she was going to bed. She then lifted both hands level in front of her, fingers curled and dancing, to indicate he could go type. He hugged her and headed down to his office, telling her he'd check on her in a couple of hours.

****

The next three hours were very productive for Randy. Jordan rested upstairs. Peace had been restored between them, however fragile, and they were together. Free to work, his fingers blazed on the keyboard, recording what he'd mentally written that morning. He added elements he hadn't anticipated and even watched as his main character made some dreadful decisions. But in the end, he felt the story would be better for them.

Randy glanced at the clock to find it was two-thirty. The boys would be home in half an hour. He'd been willing to skip lunch, but what about Jordan? Thinking he'd just finish the scene he was typing and head upstairs, Randy was shocked to soon hear the boys tromping up the stairs of the front deck. He punched save and went to greet them, shushing their boisterousness as they clomped in coated with snow.

"Let's get you guys a snack and then you can play in the rec room," he said, aware how quiet his own voice was.

But Jordan sat in the living room, just up the stairs from the front door. Silently, she scanned pages of handwritten letters. Randy glanced over, attempting a smile. She met his gaze and then motioned him toward her.

He sent the boys to the kitchen. "Find some apples, boys."

When he reached the recliner, she stretched her arms toward him and he bent to hug her. He had to drop to his knees beside her chair to better reach her. She held on for several moments and Randy felt his mouth go dry. She rarely displayed affection like this. He tried to straighten, but she held him, touching her cheek to his. He reached for her face and finally pulled back. "You okay?"

She nodded.

"I wish you could talk to me." He glanced at the letters. "You found them. We need to talk about these."

She nodded again, her fingers in the hair at his neckline. In the next moment, she wrinkled her eyebrows.

"What?" Randy toyed with the idea of bringing her a pen and pad of paper.

"Is it okay...?" she rasped.

"Please don't try to talk. Remember what Dr. Benson said? A raging infection, remember? No talking."

She pointed at the letter on her lap and then at her chest.

"I don't mind you reading those, Jae," Randy said. "But we're going to have to talk about them soon."

She looked worried again.

He smoothed her brow. "No worries. I just want to find out what you're thinking. Right now, though, I want you to rest. Are you feeling okay?" He touched her forehead. "You're warm. Let's take your temperature."

She produced the thermometer from the end table and dutifully pressed the button before putting it under her arm. They'd long ago agreed to this method of temperature taking, since washing the thing over and over again to dispel with oral germs was such a hassle.

"Want some orange juice?"

She nodded and Randy set off for the kitchen. The boys were munching away on some apples. He poured them milk and took a glass of OJ to Jordan in time to hear the digital gadget beeping. She grimaced at the numbers and then turned it to show him.

"One hundred degrees, again, huh?" He glanced at his watch. "Time for more medicine and a nap."

She toted her juice to the bedroom while he followed with Tylenol.

****

That afternoon, he was able to nearly finish his rough draft. Then, he'd sit with a red pen and a critical eye. Hopefully he'd have enough distance to see the work objectively. He could also try to find an impartial person to edit who could get started on the first half right away. He scanned his memory. One of his writing friends had mentioned someone local. He'd email him and get back to his final three or so chapters.

He was typing his missive to that friend when Cassidy and Aaron burst into the room. "Daddy! Mommy needs you."

Chapter Seven

Randy took the stairs two at a time. He found Jordan sitting in bed, tears streaming down her face. Randy sent the boys to the rec room for a family video, assuring them he would help Mommy. They left with quiet backward glances, and Randy knelt beside Jordan.

"What is it, honey? What happened? Are you okay?"

He reached toward the nightstand and pulled the box of tissues over. Then he pulled out two and handed them to her.

She took them but shook her head.

"Man, I wish you could talk. What happened?" he asked again.

After a shaky breath, she handed him a few pages she'd torn from her journal. The pale blue swirls and ragged edges testified of their origin. "What?" he wondered. She just indicated he should read the pages—a letter from her.

Randy sat back on his heels and skimmed the pages. Maybe she couldn't speak right now, but her heart was right here on the page for him to see.

Dear Randy,

Thank you for taking care of me. You came home. I really wanted you to; I needed you and you came. All of these beautiful letters, where you so easily shared exactly how you were feeling, have made me want to share, too. But, as I started to write, I wasn't sure where to begin. What do you do when you've spent nine years hiding?

I've been hiding. I wanted to blame you, but it's me. I'm the one who doesn't know how to love you. I'm the one guarding her heart. As I read these letters I see that.

Randy looked up from the pages in his hands and started to speak, but she shushed him and pointed back to the letter. He dropped his head again, finding his place.

I'm sorry for every heartache I've caused you. These letters...I wish I'd read them earlier. Everything shifts into perspective. Your distance. Your carefulness. But your feelings for me are right here, too, and I am amazed. I am undone.

Randy couldn't read any further without telling her. But when he glanced up, those tears in her eyes stopped him. It was as if she *needed* to believe what she did about them. How could he abolish her hope?

She tilted her head, sniffed and mouthed the word "what?"

"I need to explain a lot of things to you. Problem is you're sick and I've got this deadline with the novel. If I don't finish it, Carl is going to have my head."

Jordan grabbed the pages of her letter back. She turned over the final sheet and scribbled: *But...what about you and me?*

"I'm sorry, Jae. I want to stay right here, but I'm waiting for an editor to get back to me on email. He's going to check over my work. I've gotta finish my last three chapters and shoot them to him, too. Then, I need to make all the changes and I only have a couple weeks." He shook his head, again thinking how impossible it was.

Her pen scratched the back of the page again: *But...what about us? What about figuring this out?*

Randy rubbed his scratchy chin. Should he reveal the secret now, or wait? He decided to wait. Later, they could delve into the truth together and he could help her understand. And, if her laryngitis was gone, she could communicate with him, too.

"Jae, you're going to have to trust me. I have more to explain, but I really can't until after I meet this deadline." He took the letter from her hands. "I think you should rest and put this whole thing aside until you're feeling better." He climbed up from the floor; helping her move so he could sit beside her. He wrapped his arm around her and she leaned against him, her sniffles silenced. For a moment, he let himself enjoy the warm feel of her there, surrendered to his chest.

"We have a lot to talk about. I want to and we will. I need to ask you to be patient—" she let out a quick breath of resistance, but he motored ahead "—and trust that I love you. Can you do that?"

He pulled back and tipped his head to see her face. She wouldn't meet his eyes. "I love you, Jae. I really do. I want to talk about your letter, but right now isn't the best time, since you can't speak." He paused, feeling a lump form in his throat. "Your words meant a lot to me."

She cupped her ear, which he interpreted to mean that she was listening so why not talk now? He shook his head. Her gaze fell to the blankets and she didn't respond, not that he expected her to speak. The veil of resistance falling back into place stung. His cell phone began vibrating in his pocket. He quenched a sigh and reached for it. Jordan pulled back and met his gaze. He accepted the call and said, "Hello," as he disengaged himself and stood.

****

Jordan watched him take the call, hearing a mumble on the other end of the line.

Randy bent to kiss the top of her head and indicate she should lie down again. She obliged. He waved and left the room, still chatting away, probably with Carl.

Where was this elusive *R* of the letters?

Passionate, tender, loving and unafraid to share his heart, especially with *J*? Reading the notes stirred so much in her heart, sending her off to fall in love with him again. Writing him back seemed a rather fitting response, but he hadn't reacted the way she'd hoped he would. It was as if he compartmentalized himself. And right now, the center of his focus was this loathsome book deadline.

But her tears...they were a result of that undoing she'd mentioned in her note to him. She'd been crying over their relationship when Cassidy came in to see how she was feeling. Seeing her tears had excited both the twins who had chased off to locate Randy.

He'd gone back downstairs, so, obviously, he still wasn't willing to put everything else on hold to work on their marriage. She'd been vulnerable in her letter, hoping it would be the catalyst for a heart-to-heart conversation. At least he hadn't taken it with him. She felt too exposed knowing he could read it again at any time. Jordan glanced around. Where was it? She'd grabbed it back, writing something on the reverse side. Had to be here somewhere. It'd probably drifted to the floor. She'd look for it later. Crying over what they'd missed in their nine married years had drained the last of her energy. Fatigue swept over her, pulling her under. She lay back and succumbed, sleeping within moments.

****

Randy sat in his office re-reading Jordan's letter. He'd emailed the bulk of his manuscript to Ron and knew he'd bought some time. The editor would be reading and editing those pages for a while.

Jordan hadn't spared any sentiment in her prose. Was Randy right to wait to tell her the whole story? He wasn't sure. But he knew she must be feeling very drained from the infection. Dr. Benson said she'd be feeling better in a few days as the medicine worked against the germs. But he hadn't promised when she'd be able to talk again.

Jordan wrote of grieving their past, how it pained her that they'd skirted the issues of the heart all these years. She expressed regret over never truly opening up to him and wished he could just once have shared his heart with her. A lump formed in his throat as he found the truth in her words.

Maybe these letters were the perfect way to open the lines of communication. Surely God knew what He was doing. Randy had prayed about God leading them together, and sure enough, He was at the task right now. The very thought humbled Randy and he bowed his head.

"Father, heal our relationship completely, please. Bring us closer through love, expressed and enjoyed. Give each of us courage as You heal our heartaches." He pondered his original plan and decided that, too, would have to wait. But...

Standing, Randy quickly walked out to the garage. The temperature was considerably cooler in here. He positioned himself just right and peered up. Yes. Everything was still the same. Good.

Back in his office, Randy tucked Jordan's letter in his desk drawer under toner refills for his printer and resumed typing. Two more chapters and he'd be finished.

Chapter Eight

Ron had massacred his manuscript. After a weekend of writing, Randy found an email from Ron. Just that morning, Randy had sent off the rest of the manuscript with a sense of elation and concern. Hopefully, the story was as good as he thought it was.

Ron apparently hadn't thought so and had butchered it. All the changes the word-processing software marked looked like battle wounds, tied up in reddened bandages. Words deleted, *scenes* deleted. Chapters switched in order. Not to mention scene ideas inserted. This editor hadn't spared any criticism and his short email message didn't assuage Randy's own wounds.

You've got a good start. Needs a bit of touch-up. Hope this is helpful. Let me know if I can do anything else. I'll get those last chapters to you by tomorrow at noon.

Great. Another bloodbath to anticipate.

Though it was still early in the day, Randy felt weariness crowding in and pressing down on him. He attributed it to the pressures of the day. But by eight p.m., after a day of working despite interruptions of family, Randy couldn't help dragging himself off to bed.

The alarm sounded much too early the next morning, and Randy rolled out of bed to get the boys ready for school.

They prepared quietly, as was becoming the standard. Randy made himself some toast and washed it down his scratchy throat with the sting of orange juice. He got the boys on the bus and threw salt on the stairs of the front deck. They'd iced over the previous night.

When he peeked in on Jordan, she wasn't in bed. Assuming she was in the bathroom, he sat down on the bed to wait so he could see how she was feeling.

****

Two hours later, Jordan shook Randy's shoulder. "You okay, honey?" she whispered.

He forced his eyes open, trying to orient himself. When he tried to speak, his voice wouldn't cooperate. Jordan put a hand to his forehead and frowned before turning away. Randy shot a glance at the clock and threw back the covers. An ache throughout his body opposed his movements, but he had work to do. Why wouldn't his joints cooperate?

Jordan returned to the bedside with the thermometer and reached for his shirt. She lifted the fabric and he pulled it back down. Though his voice was scratchy, he informed her, "I'm not sick, just a little fatigued. After that nap, I should be fine. Time to get to work."

Jordan stayed directly in front of him. She thrust the thermometer at him and waited for him to take it and administer the test on his own. Randy finally acquiesced and put the offensive—and cold—thing under his arm. He'd just prove he didn't have a fever and she'd have to let him get to his office downstairs.

Jordan reached for his forehead while they awaited the beep. "You're hot," she rasped.

He wanted to ask her how she was feeling, but his voice wouldn't cooperate. Finally, the crazy thing beeped. He pulled it out and read it. *Great.*

Jordan snatched it from him. "One hundred point six?" she croaked. "Time for medicine and rest. I'll call the doctor."

****

They spent the afternoon at Dr. Benson's office and the pharmacy, though Randy complained about not being home to work. Again, the doctor ordered a throat culture, but since Jordan's came back positive for strep, he'd been rather confident Randy's would too. He started Randy on the same antibiotic as Jordan and sent them home. Randy tried to protest when Dr. Benson recommended bed rest until he felt better, but the doctor warned him against trying to speak.

Jordan insisted Randy rest that afternoon, despite his protestations. The problem was his body was in cahoots with Jordan, because he couldn't seem to fight the inclination to lie down and let himself sleep off the pain and fever.

Jordan saw to the boys' needs after three and Randy slept until evening.

By seven that evening, Randy was awake and his fever had broken. He was determined to at least bring his laptop to bed so he could work there. He and Jordan had been communicating in whispers and with notepads, both of them fighting this infection. So far the boys were feeling fine, though a little rambunctious without the kind of supervision their parents usually provided. Finally, Jordan corralled them into their bedroom and ordered them to ready for bed.

Meanwhile, Randy had gone for his laptop and notepad. He returned and tucked himself in, sitting against the headboard. He had multiple chapters to fix, changes to determine, entire scenes to invent. Some of Ron's recommendations weren't agreeable to Randy. He figured that was standard. But most of the others, he conceded would help. So, he began plunking away where he'd left off.

Jordan came in just after eight-thirty and slipped into bed, turning her back to him. Hopefully she could sleep with his lamp on.

By eleven, Randy's body was aching again. He distractedly checked his own temperature and wasn't surprised it had risen to 101.9. He swallowed IB in the bathroom and brushed his teeth. At least he was a little mobile. But, how his body and throat ached. Is this what Jordan had been talking about on Sunday? Fatigue and a sore throat? He felt his features droop. And he'd made her miserable, all that banging around. *Then* he'd left the kitchen in a state of fiasco. His petty frustration that afternoon seemed embarrassingly childish right now. He wanted to apologize.

Randy settled back in bed and grabbed his notepad. His pen slipped over the page with practiced strokes, his heart bobbing to the surface as he wrote.

****

Ironic, Randy thought. Communication had been the challenge of their marriage, their relationship. Yet now, when they were both really ready to try, they were each rendered practically mute by an infection. What if, when they were strong again, they found themselves just as heart- and tongue-tied as before their illnesses? Or maybe the delay would help them craft just the right words, not to mention motivating them to work through this. He hoped the latter would be true. With Jordan lying there tonight, sleeping with her back to him, he wondered. He'd never shown her the letters before. Maybe she'd thought he'd been hiding them.

At midnight, he slouched down into bed and let himself give in to the fuzzy places the medicine was taking him.

Chapter Nine

Jordan was finally feeling better. Thank God for antibiotics. She'd taken the letters back to Randy's office and replaced them in their box. So far they still hadn't truly discussed them. Questions lingered, but she'd put them on hold just like Randy had been doing.

The strep infection had taken its toll on both her emotions and her thoughts. She had struggled to string two coherent ideas together this week. Reading those letters had given her hope. Hope that perhaps Randy actually hid passion in his heart after all. And as she read, her own heart had been stirred, awakened once more. She couldn't remember when it had happened the first time. Maybe it never had. Melancholy surrounded her. Randy wasn't the one to blame for that.

Nevertheless, they'd made a commitment so they had to try. She replayed the scene when she'd let Randy read her note. He hadn't seemed upset about her having found the letters. But he hadn't seemed thrilled, either. It's the secret he hinted at that left such confusion. When would he be willing to discuss that? After the twelfth?

Perhaps. And that would be good timing, with Valentine's Day so close at hand—their tenth wedding anniversary.

Meanwhile, it was time to see how Randy was feeling this morning. He'd been adamant about meeting his ridiculous deadline. Jordan felt he should just call Carl and break the news to him about being sick and unable to make the cut-off date. But, he still had several days, so perhaps he could do it. She knew what it would do for his ego if he accomplished this goal.

An interesting thought occurred to her. What if instead of coaxing him to give up, she supported him instead? Sure, she could see the folly. But, in his shoes, she'd want support even if things didn't work out. This new strategy seemed messier, especially when experience told her they were looking at the impossible. But so what? His not making the deadline didn't reflect on her, even if she supported him. Why shouldn't she encourage his trying to keep his word to Carl?

A paradigm shift began to occur in her mind. She'd start by being encouraging, rather than negative. She'd noticed Randy had made some changes, starting with his return from the cabin. Being an encourager was a change she herself could make. The proof would be evident sooner or later. She asked God for grace as she went searching for him.

Randy was sitting up in bed with his laptop perched on his lap. His fingers clicked away on the keyboard, though he did raise one hand in a half-hearted wave when she entered. She grabbed clothes and headed for the shower. The boys wouldn't be home for hours. Thankfully, they still appeared symptom-free.

Jordan imagined Randy joining her as the water sent steam billowing around her. He'd quietly open the bathroom door, slip out of his clothes and step into the shower. She'd be surprised, because he rarely did that, instead using her shower time as an opportunity to get things done. But she'd be very glad he'd joined her. So what if he couldn't speak? Being near him would be especially sweet. But, without having worked through her questions and their past, would that shower experience be everything it could be? Did she even want him there at that moment, knowing they hadn't talked through their heart issues?

Suddenly it didn't matter. Jordan's heart rate kicked up.

Randy had just entered the bathroom.

Now, of course, he could have come in to take care of other needs. But, a part of her deeply hoped, risky though it was, that he was there to be with her.

She closed her eyes and rinsed the shampoo out of her hair, determined to keep her heart locked up safe and sound. So what if he didn't join her? His mind was probably so focused on his writing that the fact she stood there only slightly obscured by the steamy glass of the shower probably hadn't meant much to him. Not after nine years. People shower. Everyday. It doesn't have to be more than just a means to cleanliness.

Of course, she could take the risk of asking him to join her. Jordan considered that a minute. What if he refused? It struck her that being unwilling to take risks hadn't helped their marriage. But her courage had taken cover. Shame coated her heart when she realized she hadn't even been willing to do what she'd judged Randy for. She still hadn't opened up.

In the next instant, her breath caught in her throat. Randy opened the shower door, but he was still clothed. "Sorry," he said on a ragged whisper. "I can't find any more ibuprofen." His sheepish expression would have been cute except for their predicament.

Jordan thought a moment, resisting the urge to hide, especially since there was nowhere to go. "In the pantry, I think," she said, her voice still sounded a bit scratchy, even to her.

"Thanks," Randy said and closed the door, leaving her alone. Obviously he had a one-track mind at this moment and it was solely focused on pain relief.

So be it.

Jordan finished her shower and toweled off. When she peered around the bathroom door, she found Randy had left the bedroom. She let tears roll down her face. How she wanted to feel like a priority to him. Of course she knew he cared, at some level. He had, after all, come home from the cabin when he found out she really was sick. She released a shaky breath. How she wanted him to demonstrate it to her, with more than just a shared shower. They had nearly a decade of deep affection to make up for.

Randy's big deadline was nearly upon them and everything else in their lives was on hold. He didn't have much of his voice, and he hadn't explained whatever secret lurked around the letters. She was determined to try harder, to clear up previous misunderstandings, and just maybe risk opening her own heart. She wanted to work on their relationship. But Randy seemed disengaged, focusing mostly on his book, leaving her feeling empty.

****

The Monday before Randy's deadline, Jordan started back to work. Her time wasn't consumed by her work like Randy's. This close to his cut-off date, he'd barricaded himself in his office, shutting the rest of the family out.

Jordan returned from work just before dinner and headed directly to their bedroom to change before preparing dinner. The boys sounded like they were destroying the rec room. She'd have to check on them soon since Randy obviously wasn't feeling responsible for them tonight. Jordan traipsed down the stairs to find their sons. They'd managed to pull the curtains down from the wall, rod and all, and two pillows lay shrouded in fluff. Some of the white stuffing was still settling when she walked in with her hands on her hips. "Aaron! Cassidy! What are you doing?"

Each boy stopped mid-rampage across the cushion-less sofas.

"Clean this up and get upstairs for some dinner."

The boys attempted to wipe smirks from their faces, Jordan noticed, as they got to work.

Jordan turned toward her husband's home office. She tapped once and opened the door. "Randy, the boys have torn that room apart." She pointed over her shoulder. "Couldn't you hear them?"

Randy hunched over his computer; he barely seemed to be breathing. His fingers tapped on the keyboard, moving almost as quickly as his darting eyes.

"Randy?"

"Hm?" he grunted.

"Oh, never mind." She turned and stalked back to check on the boys before mounting the stairs once more for dinner. Tonight seemed like a sloppy joes kind of night. Quick and easy preparation. She got to work browning the hamburger.

If Randy hadn't even noticed the boys wrecking the house, he wouldn't notice anything. It was a good thing nothing tragic or urgent had happened. A plan began to form in her mind. What if she and the boys left for a couple of days? He probably wouldn't notice that either. Staying here was wearing on her because Randy hadn't even communicated two words to her. She'd decided to be supportive. Sure. But sane, too. He was holed up in that office of his night and day. Had he even come to bed last night? She hadn't seen him there last night or this morning when she'd gotten up for work. But, somehow he had gotten the boys ready and out the door to the bus. Miracle of miracles.

So, maybe she'd take the boys and head to their favorite hotel. She could enjoy some relaxation in their hot tub and the boys could go swimming. She could also try to forget she wasn't very high on her husband's priority list.

After church on Sunday the 11th, which Randy didn't even attend though he was feeling better, Jordan and the twins set out for the hotel. Although she doubted he would find it, she stuck a note on the refrigerator for Randy. All afternoon and evening, she never heard from him.

She drove the boys to school on Monday the twelfth, and then headed in to work. Her cell phone remained silent. No calls from Randy. Glancing out her office's window, Jordan didn't relish the thought of tackling the shining parking lot and those glistening streets in order to pick up the boys soon. She left extra time, knowing the twenty-five minute drive would likely be extended.

****

Carl began calling at noon on the twelfth.

Randy had sat on the edge of his chair all morning, reading his screen as fast as he could and changing nearly every scene. He'd caught a two-hour nap the previous night on the sofa in the rec room. He still had a third of the manuscript to review when he answered Carl's second call at one p.m.

"Do you want the first half?"

"I want the whole thing."

Randy rubbed his neck. "Polished or shoddy?"

"I'd settle for somewhere in between at this point."

"It's on its way."

At three o'clock, Randy attached his manuscript file to an email message and shot it off to Carl with an accompanying phone call.

Then he collapsed against the back of his chair and took his first deep breath in a week.

He'd done it!

Time to find Jordan and celebrate. He took the stairs two at a time, adrenaline coursing through him. He called Jordan's name, but she didn't answer. She wasn't in the house. He dialed her cell phone and she didn't pick up. Finally, he checked the garage and found her van missing.

Three-fifteen. Maybe she was getting the boys. He called their school. Sure enough, she had been there at three to meet them. Randy didn't want to listen to the office attendant's cute story, but remained on the line, all the while searching his thoughts for where Jordan might be.

"...that's when Cassidy started talking about going swimming. 'In this weather? You must have an indoor pool,' I told him. But he said it was the hotel's and they were just borrowing it for a couple of days."

A hotel? Randy thanked the woman and clicked off. Had he really neglected his family so severely he'd missed their leaving for a hotel?

Randy tugged on a coat and climbed into his truck. He'd start with Jordan's favorite nearby getaway spot.

Hail pelted his pick-up as soon as he exposed it to the elements. He wondered how many dents he'd find after this excursion. Visibility was limited, but the most challenging aspect was slick roads. He nearly lost control twice on his way to the highway.

Crews worked to salt the two-lane, but ice built up despite their efforts. Randy clutched the wheel tightly, deciding if he did find Jordan at a hotel, they'd all stay there until this system had passed. They could call it a little post-deadline getaway.

She had probably just driven this stretch, coming from the boys' school and driving toward the hotel. Hopefully, she'd beaten this storm.

Ten minutes later, he pulled off to let a fire truck pass. Shortly after that an ambulance whirred past as well. Randy's pulse quickened. His mind entertained dire circumstances, all involving his wife's minivan, a spinout and a rescue effort.

It took an eternity to come upon the accident. The vow Randy had made while still at the cabin ran through his mind and he determined—again—to follow through, if he had the chance.

Yes. His deadline had taken first priority, but only for a short time. Now he was free to focus on them. Why couldn't Jordan have given him another day? He'd met his deadline but did that even matter any more? Not if Jordan and the boys were hurt, or worse.

She'd never gotten to see his true heart in all these years. What good had his guards done if they had cost him the love of Jordan?

That would be one of his biggest regrets, if...

Oh, God, please...

He'd show her if by God's mercy he still could.

Randy spotted the accident site directly in front of him, as he peered past the busily swiping wiper blades. He eased up on the accelerator. A rescue worker headed over the crest on foot into the ditch causing Randy to pray again that Jordan and the twins were okay.

That's when he recognized their van.

Chapter Ten

Randy slid toward the emergency vehicles on the side of the road, hoping he wouldn't collide with them. He turned his wheel in the direction of the fire engine and felt his truck slowly glide in that direction. Helpless, he held the wheel and waited. Thankfully he stopped in time.

Randy climbed out and moved to the side of the road, peering over the edge. A pickup laid upside-down in the ravine. Crews were working on the driver's door. Jordan was nowhere in sight. Randy walked along the edge of the ditch. When he came around the side of the fire truck, he saw Jordan standing with a police officer. Finally, he could let himself exhale. Her van was parked beyond the ambulance and police car. The boys weren't outside with her but she looked okay. No injuries that he could make out. And from here, the van looked unscathed.

He approached, listening to the officer's voice. When Jordan spotted him, her gaze darted back to his for a double take. "Randy?"

"Jordan. Are you all right?"

The police officer turned, pad in his gloved

hands. He squinted against the blowing snow. "Who's this?"

"My husband."

"I saw your van. Are you all right?"

"I'm fine."

"She's giving a report. We'll only be another few moments. Please stand back away from the road," the officer instructed.

Randy's breath circled around his head as he stepped further onto the shoulder. Thankfully the sleet had let up. Now, wet flakes fell. Seems they could have conducted this interview inside the patrolman's car. Randy bounced on his feet, shoving his hands deeper into his pockets. The wind assaulted his face. He guessed the temperature hovered right at freezing.

Finally, the officer disengaged from her and Randy stepped up. "Are the boys okay?" He wanted to surround her with his arms, to kiss her until they were both warm again. He wanted to express how worried he'd been when he came upon the accident minutes ago.

"They're in the van."

Randy pulled his hands from his jacket pockets and debated his next action. In his mind's eye he stepped very close to Jordan and grasped her elbows. Snow whipped around their heads, but Randy didn't care. He pulled her closer and watched surprise flicker in her gaze. She nervously glanced around. He tugged her even closer and met her mouth with his.

Jordan's words broke into his thoughts. "I wanted to keep them out of danger."

"Good move," Randy said, crossing his arms over his chest. The moment passed and once again, he hadn't acted on it.

She started toward her van and he followed. The boys were steaming up the back window. They'd each written their names in the fog. Cassidy tumbled out first when Jordan opened the slider. Aaron was right behind. They each hugged Randy.

"Are you coming with us to the hotel, Dad?"

Randy didn't even look at Jordan. "Yes."

"Great!"

"Yippee!"

He met Jordan's gaze and saw a mixture of apprehension and interest. This was one instance he'd have his way.

"I'll be right behind you, Jae," he said after the boys had climbed back in and he'd closed the slider.

If only he'd thought to bring the box with him. Randy berated himself. He'd been too distraught by the weather and Jordan's disappearance to think twice about anything except starting out after her.

And thankfully, she was okay.

So what, he didn't have what he needed? Jordan and the boys were safe. There'd be time later for his secret.

"Ready or not, Jordan. I'm coming after you," he spoke in the quiet of the truck cab as he eased onto the highway behind Jordan's van.

Chapter Eleven

The Ambrose family spilled into their hotel room. Jordan hadn't said much since they'd arrived at the hotel. Randy hoped she wouldn't be this silent their entire stay, now that he could talk again.

The boys found a clean hour of sitcom reruns on cable and Randy took the remote control with him to find Jordan. She'd escaped to the bedroom.

He closed the door behind him. "Jae. What's going on?"

She glanced up at him from the edge of the bed.

Randy sat beside her. She inched away from him.

He felt his eyebrows crinkle. "What?"

"I'm through not being a priority."

"You *are* my priority, Jae. That's why I'm here."

Jordan reached up and fingered an earring.

"I just had to finish up that novel by its deadline."

"Right."

"But, I did it, Jae. I finished it."

"I bet you didn't even notice I was gone until you were done," she griped.

Randy felt a sheepish expression steal over his face. His posture slumped. "I didn't. You're right."

"Even though it was overnight?" She sounded incredulous.

"I worked through the night, caught a catnap on the sofa in the rec room somewhere around two." He reached for her shoulder. "I'm sorry. Jae, listen, when I saw your van at the accident site today, I was terrified."

"Why?" she challenged him.

"Because I don't think I can live without you."

She eyed him, looking surprised. Then she pulled away.

"Why do you do that?"

"What?"

"Pull away."

She shrugged.

Randy stood and moved to the window where he drew back the sheers then the heavy drapes. Finally he turned. She'd been watching him. It was now or never. He drew in a deep breath. "I need to show you something."

She tilted her head. "Okay."

Randy swallowed, hating the risks in this conversation, in his new determination. "Um… actually, it's back at home."

"What is?"

"I need to show you in person."

Jordan settled her hands on the bed behind her, locked her elbows and leaned back. "I'm tired of playing games, Randy."

"I know. I have a lot of explaining to do and I will. Now that the book is in to Carl, I'm free for a while, Jae. Let's celebrate. Let's work on our relationship." Randy walked over to where she sat on the bed and held out his hands. She glanced at them, but didn't move to take them. "You won't even try?" Randy's voice caught.

She grimaced, obviously attempting to control her emotions. She pressed her lips together to still their twitching. "Trying wears me out."

"I know. But I want to try. I want to show you."

Jordan looked away, grabbed a long breath. "Pardon me if I don't get excited."

Defeat pounded against Randy's heart as he saw the work cut out for him.

Aaron burst into the bedroom, requesting dinner. Jordan rose and met the boys in the kitchenette. Randy followed, inspecting the bedroom door for a lock on his way by.

"We're going to have to call room service," Jordan declared.

"Why don't we just go home?" Randy asked. "The storm's let up."

Cassidy yanked back the curtain overlooking the grounds. "Look daddy! The rain's coming sideways again."

Randy watched the sleet slice toward the

glass. "Well, so much for going home tonight."

"We're booked through tonight anyway," Jordan said.

"Let's stay, Daddy. The swimming pool is great! But Mommy spends most of her time in the hot tub."

Randy cocked his head at Jordan. "She does, does she?"

Both boys nodded. Jordan's color shifted hues.

"Then, I've got an idea. Let's order a pizza. The restaurant's just down the street. I imagine they can run one over. Then, after we eat, and rest a while, we can hit the swimming pool and..." he eyed Jordan, "the hot tub."

The boys cheered. Jordan studied him, and Randy couldn't stop a grin. Hot tub, indeed.

****

The family slouched over the coffee table watching one of their favorite animated movies while they ate up the pizza some brave deliveryman had brought to their door. Randy tipped him well, considering his trek.

"Okay, boys, clean up this mess," Randy directed after they'd finished the last slice. The boys groaned, but Randy cleared his throat and the twins quietly got to work. "Half an hour to the pool."

"That was a pretty big meal, Randy. We'd better give them forty-five minutes."

"Sure. By the time we get changed and head down there it'll probably be close to seven."

"Do you think we'll have school tomorrow, Daddy?"

"I don't know! Maybe not and we could party all night," Randy joked.

Aaron hollered, "Woo hoo!"

"Don't get them all worked up," Jordan scolded.

"We're not worked up, are we boys? We're celebrating!" He high-fived his kids. "Daddy met his deadline!"

Cassidy darted to the sofa where he jumped up on the cushions.

"Okay, Cass. Down you go," Randy said. "Mom's right. We gotta keep ourselves under control. Who wants to come with me to the gift shop and help me find some swimming trunks?"

"I do!" both boys chorused.

Randy stepped over to Jordan. "I didn't bring anything with me, just jumped into the car and came looking for you."

She glanced up into his eyes.

Her vulnerable look invited him to touch her, but he held back. Instead, he softened his voice to an intimate tone. "Promise you won't go anywhere while I'm gone?"

She swallowed. "I won't."

"Promise?"

A hint of a grin threatened. "Promise. I'm too full, anyway. I think I'll watch the news."

Randy took the boys down to the gift shop moments later.

****

Jordan scanned the channels, settling on a romantic movie instead of the news. She joined the story at a particularly passionate scene. The actors maintained their clothing, but their kisses stole Jordan's breath. She watched the leading male lace his fingers into the actress's hair. The heroine tried to pull away, though Jordan couldn't imagine why she'd want to. The hero tugged her back into his space, covering her mouth with his. She pushed against him, but predictably traded in struggling for a moan moments later.

Why didn't Randy ever act like that? The bigger question was: what would she do if he ever did? Romance wasn't Randy's strong suit. Sure, there were times he could get riled up a bit, but those times were rare. It wasn't as if Randy never pursued her; they had twin sons to prove that. It was more that he didn't let himself lose control. In their marriage, she'd learned that they could make love often, but not truly connect, not truly be passionate and free with each other. They could be totally undressed together, but remain totally guarded.

Randy seemed to avoid the stronger emotions. Considering his upbringing, she could understand his carefulness where anger or rage was concerned. But passion? He kept himself tightly reigned in, never feeling anything very deeply, or at least, so she could perceive it. Just once she'd like to see him get riled up.

Maybe that's why she pushed him.

She also resisted him. Like in the bedroom tonight. He'd actually been reaching toward her, heart and all, but she'd only turned a cold shoulder. How often had she done that? Too often. She grimaced. It was easier to blame their problems on Randy.

Watching the characters pretend to enjoy each other at a deeper level, Jordan felt a familiar ache in her heart. Intimacy could change everything. Randy's ardor would ignite the fire she craved but the full opening of his heart would be the refreshing water her soul needed. She had a hunch if he could get in touch with anger, maybe he'd connect with passion, too. But she also feared what he'd loose if he ever did. Or what he'd find in her.

****

When Randy returned to their room, he found a note.

I didn't leave. I'm in the hot tub...waiting for my family.

Randy directed the boys to change as quickly as they could and meet him in a few minutes. He stepped into his room, stripped out of his clothes, and pulled on his new trunks. Thankfully, the gift shop carried swimwear, despite the frigid outdoor temperatures. Then he yanked on a complimentary robe and slipped on his shoes.

All the way to the poolroom, Randy mused over Jordan's note. She'd made a blatant invitation, drawing him like a fly to honey with her hot tub comment. When they arrived, the hot tub was empty. Randy's gaze darted around the room.

"She's in the pool," Cassidy observed. "Hi, Mommy!"

Each boy leapt up and curled into a ball before dropping into the water. The Ambrose family was alone in the room, for now.

Randy lowered himself slowly into the hot tub while watching Jordan make another lap and the boys splash around. The water was hotter than he'd expected. Maybe that was why Jordan had opted for the pool instead.

"You coming over?" Randy called when Jordan stopped at the closest side of the pool.

She pulled herself up so that her whole face was visible over the edge. "Why don't you come over here?"

"I'm just getting used to this," Randy said, sitting for the first time.

She slipped back in. "Well, I'm going to do another lap."

"Okay." *But I miss you.*

Randy watched her.

Oh, Jae. If only you knew how many times I've held back. How many letters I've composed to you. Honey, come over here so I can whisper in your ear. Let me hold you close, trail kisses down your neck.

Of course, he could go to her, chase her through the water. Catch her. Trap her against the side of the pool, encase her in his arms. Kiss her wet face until she was breathless. The twins were a consideration, but not in the vivid images running through his mind.

Randy's heart thumped in his chest. When he imagined her reaction, the images faded. She could reject him like she'd done so often in their marriage.

Randy sat back and let the hot water work it's magic on his body, relaxing muscles he'd tensed for months. Yes, this was just what he needed after fulfilling his obligations to Carl and his contract.

Moments later, Jordan splashed Randy's chest with pool water, startling his eyes open.

He grinned. "What was that for?"

She stood over him. "You looked like you were about to fall asleep. Not a very safe idea, Mr. Ambrose."

"No?" he asked, reaching for her ankle. "I think you should come in here and keep me awake."

She screeched and jumped before he could grab her. "Nope."

He made a show of groping at the concrete. "Whatya mean, 'nope'?"

"I'm heading back to the room." She stepped away.

Randy watched her in her well-fitting one-piece suit while his mind conjured an image of launching himself at her and grasping her arms. "Come sit with me," he would implore, while meeting her gaze. The twins might distract him for a minute, but they could play in the pool with a beach ball. Randy would spare them a quick glance before wrapping an arm around Jordan and escorting her to the hot tub.

But in reality, he stayed seated and calm. He hated always wimping out, but there was no precedent in their relationship for any kind of ardent demands from him. Instead, he resorted to pleading. "C'mon, Jae. Join me. For a minute or two."

Jordan looked over at the boys. They played happily. Apparently she didn't find any excuse for not doing so. "Okay." Slowly, she dipped her toes into the water. "This is hot."

"You'll get used to it."

Finally, she sat beside him. He draped an arm behind her, and she looked over at him. "I do wanna try, Randy."

He pulled her closer and she rested her head against his shoulder. "Me, too. We don't have to settle, you know, not with God in this with us. I want to talk things through."

"Then we can't judge each other."

"Exactly."

"Is this something I'm going to have to keep in mind when you show me whatever it is you have to show me?"

Randy chuckled. "It *is* kinda risky."

She pulled back. "How so?"

"You'll see. Just remember this conversation."

She settled back against his shoulder,

tracing patterns over his taught stomach. "I'm almost afraid to ask, but what do you want to do for Valentine's Day, our anniversary?"

Her touch stirred more than the water, but fear replaced those thoughts. He silently debated how to answer.

"You forgot."

He wrinkled his face, but wouldn't lie. "I'm sorry. We can do whatever you want." He cupped water in his hand and rained it over her exposed shoulder. "Tonight could be an early celebration of our special day."

"I can't believe you'd forget our anniversary. Again."

"C'mon, I don't usually forget. Maybe twice in ten years, I've forgotten. Anyway, I think the surprise I have waiting for you is going to make all the difference."

She watched him. "We can finally talk about the letters."

"Yup. Anytime you want." Randy turned, facing her, earnest. "You are my priority, Jae. I'm going to take a break for a couple of days from writing, through Valentine's Day. We can celebrate for 48-hours solid."

She shivered.

"What's the matter?"

"That look in your eye—" she slouched under the water "—it's kind of scary."

"Yeah?" Randy leaned forward, feeling desire reawaken inside him.

She nodded, watching him lean toward her.

"Give that back!" Cassidy stomped out of the pool, dripping with water and marched to the hot tub. "Mom! Dad! Aaron took the ball and he's hogging it."

Randy and Jordan exchanged glances. "Time to head back?"

"Yup," Jordan agreed and they dried off to go up to their room. "If they have school tomorrow, we've gotta see that they get some sleep first."

They hit the elevator. "I remember Valentine's Day in elementary school." Randy directed his question to the twins, "Did you boys make out cards for your classmates?" They nodded. "Good. It's going to be a great week." He squeezed Jordan's hand.

Chapter Twelve

Their night at the hotel never got off the ground after they returned to their room. Cassidy suffered a stomachache until after midnight and Randy stayed with him in the main room of their suite. Jordan was fast asleep when he finally came into the room. The following morning, while Jordan and the boys packed their things, Randy made a few phone calls. He arranged for Jordan's parents to host the boys, beginning tonight, for a couple of days. But first, they had to get the kids to school and Jordan to work. No stomachaches lingered, so they dropped off the boys on their way to Jordan's office.

Randy had the day to plan his own surprises. He began with an errand downtown where he could hit the jewelry store and the grocery outlet in the same trip. He bought a card and arranged for flowers to be delivered the following day around lunchtime. They'd have a special dinner tonight, and if all went well, they'd awaken to their anniversary with a healed relationship, at least for the most part.

But Jordan returned from work with a

migraine and went straight to bed. Her parents dropped by for the twins. Then, Randy spent the evening nursing Jordan in their dimly lit bedroom. She would have the next morning off if this headache didn't clear up.

****

The following day, she still battled the pain, but was able to offer him a warm smile and "happy anniversary" before asking for some space for a few more hours of rest.

She made an appearance just before the florist pulled up in a white van covered in decals to make a special delivery. Eight white roses with four red ones intermixed. Her favorite combination. She answered the door and received the box of flowers while Randy stood at the top of the stairs watching. When she climbed back up to the main level, she met his gaze.

He reached for her waist. "Happy tenth, honey."

"Thank you." She toted the box to the kitchen, read the simple card and began filling the vase Randy supplied with water. She loved arranging the roses with babies' breath. He watched her every move, cherishing their time together. When she was satisfied with the arrangement, she looked up into his eyes. "I appreciate your arranging for the boys to be with my folks after school today. That means a lot."

He nodded. "Are you feeling better?"

"Yeah, for the most part, though I feel dehydrated and need some water."

"I'll get it." Randy went to the kitchen. "I rented a movie we could watch."

"Sounds good."

"It's that romantic comedy we've been talking about renting."

She received the glass. "Thanks."

He sat beside her on the sofa and pressed on the remote.

****

Near dinnertime, Randy announced. "I'm making supper. You can rest."

She looked at him meaningfully. "Thank you, but I can help."

Randy stood at the stovetop, checking on his steaming vegetables. "Okay, how about setting the table the way you like it, with candles and whatever else you want."

"China. We have to use our wedding china."

"Right. Absolutely."

She got to work. Just before they sat down, each of them took a turn dressing up. When Randy emerged in dress slacks with a blazer over a mock turtleneck sweater, Jordan had dimmed the lights. His pulse quickened. She wore a deep red gown he hadn't seen before, a perfect choice considering one of his surprises for her. He stopped next to her chair. "You look amazing."

As she would sometimes do in their married lives when she was feeling playful, she adopted an English accent and told him, "Thank you, kind sir."

He grinned and moved toward the kitchen to serve their dinner. He spooned out wild rice and steamed broccoli with carrots into serving bowls and carried them over to the table. Last, he brought over the platter of broiled salmon.

Jordan glanced around. "This looks great."

Randy bowed before he sat. "Thank you," he said formally, making her smile. He pointed to her napkin. "May I?"

"Why thank you," she said, still playing along.

He bent and slowly opened the linen napkin they reserved for special dinners together. As he laid open the main fold, he exposed a bracelet of glittering heart-shaped garnets, lined up in a row of white gold.

She gasped. "Randy!"

He grinned. *Perfect.* "For the lady."

She reached for it and held it close for inspection. "This is beautiful." She draped it over her delicate wrist. "It matches my dress."

"Which I love, by the way."

She smiled.

"May I help you put it on?"

"Please."

Jordan admired the piece for several moments before looking up again. Her eyes sparkled. "I love it."

He smiled at her. "I'm glad."

All evening, she would glance down and

admire her gift, turning her wrist side to side. He enjoyed catching her look of childlike joy, but also a hint that some of her questions had been answered.

Randy flicked his own napkin over his lap. When it had settled, he leaned forward. "Tonight is going to be a very special night."

"It already is." Something dawned on her. "Oh, yeah. You have something you want to tell me. I completely forgot until now."

"First we eat," Randy said, dishing rice onto Jordan's plate. "Then we indulge in my secret."

"Indulge?" She wore a surprised grin.

"You'll see."

Occasionally, throughout dinner, Randy would begin to lose his resolve. He'd been given plenty of opportunities to renege on his plan since Monday. But, he kept telling himself tonight was the night. He couldn't put this off any longer. Whenever he would doubt her reaction, he reminded himself of her response to his gift. She remained open and unguarded even now. Her flirting with him helped. She hadn't done that in a long time.

"When should I get out my gift for you?"

"Whenever you want."

She stood and walked to the hall closet. There, she pulled out a box and returned to the table. "For my valentine. In honor of your first book sale." She referred to his selling the project to the publisher.

Randy's hands shook as he pulled back the

tissue paper to reveal a folded piece of heavy paper. He lifted it out. The sheet was a book jacket. His gaze shot to Jordan who grinned with pleasure.

"How did you do this?"

"Carl and I have been talking. He said it's only a mock-up. While it may not look like this when it's finished, he pulled something together to help me for our anniversary."

The sheet was glossy, like a book cover. The title of his novel appeared in large letters: "Granddad's Cabin" with his name appearing beneath the words: "A novel by." Randy couldn't catch a breath right away. Her gift meant she fully supported him after all. Tears came quickly to his eyes, but he didn't care.

"Thank you, Jae. This means a lot." He stood and moved to her side where he could catch her in a hug.

The back of the jacket was decorated in the blurb about his story, as well as a small shot of him he'd had taken at a local photography studio and his bio. Tomorrow, he'd call Carl and thank him as well.

Now that they'd finished their meal, Randy tried to lead Jordan to the sofa for the next phase of the evening. But, she told him she wanted to clean up the kitchen first. He agreed, since he had to go down to the garage for his next surprise for her. All of his earlier doubts were crumbling away.

By the time Jordan joined him in the living

room, the earlier intimacy had been replaced by a nervous anticipation. Randy waited for Jordan to sit near him on the sofa. The box he'd brought in rested at his feet. Jordan's expression showed interest, though she didn't say anything.

This was his moment.

He took her hand. "The first thing I need to tell you is…those letters you were reading a couple of weeks ago weren't written by me."

She started. Clearly she hadn't expected him to begin there. "What?"

Randy took a deep breath. "They were my inspiration. Granddad wrote them to Grandma Jillian."

"Durham? But what about the 'R'?"

"His nickname was Red, because of his hair." Randy drew Jordan's hair around in front of her shoulder.

"Oh."

He reached for her chin. "But don't be disappointed. Take a look at this box."

"I didn't see that one in your closet."

He shook his head. "It was in the attic of the garage, instead of my office." Randy handed her the first letter.

She looked at him.

"Read it."

Jordan pulled a tri-folded sheet from an unsealed envelope. The first line reminded her of the previous letters. She read on.

I have so much to tell you, so much to explain. But I could never tell you in person. I

don't know why. I just...Oh, J, even writing this is difficult. I can guess why. Makes me angry. I long for the day he doesn't shadow everything I think or my willingness to take risks. I don't know if you'll ever read this, but if you do, remember I tried the best I knew to love you.
With all my heart, Randy

Jordan noted the way he'd signed it. *Randy*. But also, "With all my heart." Red had signed "With all my love."

She glanced up at him, the letter still in her hands. "These are a little different."

He fixed his gaze on her features. Had she always been so lovely? "How so?"

"The way you sign off, for one." She paused, looked down at the letter, then back up again. "Why didn't you tell me when you caught me reading the other letters that they weren't even from you? That they weren't to me?" She sounded irritated, but also hurt, vulnerable.

"I knew I'd have a lot to explain, and right then, under all the pressure from Carl, I couldn't. I'm sorry if you're disappointed." Randy picked up the box and set it on his lap. "But these are all for you, from me." He tipped the box toward her. "Wanna read them?"

Slowly, she shook her head, refusing. "Why are you getting them out now?"

He shrugged. "Felt like I was supposed to."

"Supposed to?"

"Well, after you found the other letters...I

don't know. It just seemed like the right time." He paused and then said, "That and I think God is asking me to show them to you now."

She was shaking her head again. "I can't."

"Why not?"

Tears glistened in her eyes, but she faced him. "I'm afraid," she whispered on a ragged breath.

He set the box on the coffee table, scooted closer and took her hands. "Of what?"

She was silent.

"I've got all the time you need, Jae."

She swallowed. "I'm afraid I won't find what I'm looking for in them," she whispered.

"What are you looking for?"

Her eyebrows furled as she studied him.

"Tell me," he coaxed.

"Your heart...passion..." Her words were so quiet; he couldn't be absolutely certain what she'd said.

After several moments of silence, Randy reached for the next letter in the box. "Can I read them to you?"

"Okay," she said. In the next moment, a look of determination came over her features. She snagged his hand. He stood, trying to balance the box in one arm and chuckling as she was dragging him off. Once in the bedroom, she settled on the blankets arranging her dress around her and leaning on her side. She looked over at him expectantly.

Chapter Thirteen

Randy set the box on his nightstand and settled against the headboard to read.

He read letter after letter, displaying his heart for her inspection. The risk, the chance he was taking that she wouldn't understand or worse, she'd act indifferent to these letters made his heart clench. But he forged ahead, as if marching headlong into a windstorm. This is what God had asked him to do. God was in charge of the consequences. *But, please, God. Let this go well,* he prayed silently.

One particular letter became a turning point.

J, believe me. I adore you. I have to be careful. Even writing this, I'm about to burst. I will find you tonight. I will, when I finish writing these words, and I will show you. I will show you. I want you to believe I love you. Don't turn away. Don't deny me, don't deny us. Oh, J. When I come to you tonight, let me love you. Let me show you. I will.

She stopped him with a hand on his forearm. "Wait. When was that?"

Randy shifted the page, feigning a search for

Love Letters

a date. Granddad had never dated his and neither had Randy. "I don't know...a couple of years ago," he guessed.

"That's how you feel? How you've felt?"

Randy nodded.

She sat up, took the letter and put it behind her. "Show me."

He watched her breaths come faster. He sensed a tinge of fear mixed with anticipation.

Now what?

She waited, while he tried to work up the lion-hearted passion of that letter from years ago. He couldn't. *Lord, help me here. I feel some walls starting to weaken. What will be left if I cooperate with their falling?*

"Randy?"

He looked around the room, cleared his throat.

"Show me," she insisted.

He didn't move. She snatched the letter and began reading.

Because I'll take you in my arms. I will show you. This time, talk of the twins, dinner, or anything else won't stop me. My love will speak for me. Tenderness, J. That's what you need.

Randy reached for her and brushed a tendril of hair away from her cheek. He loved watching her recite those words. Why hadn't they done this earlier? She stirred a faint ember inside him. But touching that spark was a far cry from risking igniting it with Jordan. What kind of boundaries do you put on a three-alarm fire?

Passion and anger, two related ideas. Weren't they? If he permitted passion now, wouldn't that give anger an open door at another time? Strong emotions intimidated him since the example of his father. But, he'd given his anger toward his father over to God at the cabin. Maybe it was safe now to let himself go.

She looked up, turning her body toward his. "Well?" When he didn't answer, she leaned over and grabbed the box, dragging it close to her. She began pulling the letters out.

"Why did you hide these from me?"

He swallowed.

"You never showed them to me. Why not?"

He couldn't answer. She scanned a couple letters, analyzing them. Nervous energy compelled Randy off the bed. He began pacing.

She studied a few more, her intensity growing. Finally, she said, "You know, as I read these, I feel a little afraid. You're intimidating in these letters—wild. That's both attractive and scary to me...but I don't think it's me who's afraid," she said, looking up at him. "I think it's you."

Her accurate words stung. Randy settled into the rocking chair they'd had in their bedroom since the days of coaxing their boys back to sleep in the middle of the night. He tipped the chair back and forth, focusing on being calm. "What do you mean?"

She adjusted herself, working up her argument and her position until she was on her knees. Her dress had shifted in her movements, permitting him a stirring view he hadn't had before. Jordan earnestly searched his eyes as if she had never truly understood him, but was finally beginning to.

"Why are your feelings here on these pages instead of here?" She pointed to her heart. "If you'd shared these sentiments with me, I'd have them here. I'd hold them here." She draped her fingers over her chest. His heart beat harder.

"But you didn't. You kept them to yourself. It's like you had an affair with these pages. I know you're a writer and you like to get your feelings down on paper. But, I want you to write what you're feeling on my heart." Her voice cracked.

Randy pushed his tongue against his teeth, felt his eyes sting. He tightened his jaw.

"Why didn't you share this with me? Not the letters. Your life, your heart? What are you afraid of?"

Randy tried to speak, but tears drowned his voice. He cleared his throat. "You're right. I have been afraid. I'm not afraid anymore."

"You are," she said, defiance in her tone and her expression. "Prove you're not."

"If I am, it's because of you," he said, defensively.

Her face contorted. "What?"

He kept up this tactic, hoping it would lead somewhere but also fearing it would. "Didn't you see a pattern in those letters? Something I kept mentioning over and over again?"

"Like what?"

He waited, giving her a chance to glance at an arbitrary letter from the piles around her.

"Oh, yeah. You're always saying you wanted to *show me* your love."

He took a breath and nodded. "Exactly."

Chapter Fourteen

"Exactly?"

He leaned forward from the rocking chair. "You have never believed me. I keep telling you, have always told you, that I love you. You just don't seem to believe it."

"Believe what?"

His voice gentled as his gaze traced her features. "How much I do."

"How can I? Your heart is poured out on these pages, instead of all over me."

He swallowed again "Oh, Jae," he murmured.

She eyed him. "You know, you say that a lot in your letters. '*Oh, J.*'" She sighed, but it sounded more frustrated than amorous. "I don't hear you say that aloud very often." She dropped her voice. "What I wouldn't give to hear that whispered in my ear while you lock me in your arms."

This time Randy didn't think first.

He bolted from the old-fashioned rocker, sending it flashing backwards and cracking against the wall. He launched himself, landing in front of her on the scattered letters. He took hold of her face, his fingers in her hair as he released the clip binding it up. "You always push me to the limits, Jae." He kissed her, pressing his lips against hers, willing them to open. "I've always been so afraid you'd push me too far, or keep pushing me away," he murmured against her mouth. Silent tears escaped his eyes. God had brought it, the breakthrough that would allow him to fully risk expressing his love without fear of loosing passion, too.

She murmured amorous words, which spurred him on as he lowered her to the pillows.

Fire blazed between them. He caressed her shoulder, kissed tears from her face and worked on the zipper at her back. When she was free of the top half of her dress, she arched toward him, offering him her heart.

****

Darkness still blanketed the outdoors when Jordan turned in Randy's direction and opened her eyes. Candles flickered in various places around the room. He reached for her shoulder, ran a caress over her skin.

"Hey, I love you."

She grinned. "That's no longer in question."

"No?" He pretended disbelief.

"Uh-uh." She shook her head against the pillow, then scooted closer and turned around.

Randy wrapped her in his arms, felt her warm back press against his chest. "If I'd have known those letters would lead to all this, I'd have gotten them out years ago. Except I might not have been ready."

"Me either, but part of me wishes you had."

"Forgive me?"

She turned her head so he caught her profile. But he could hear her better. "Just start telling me in person, Randy. That's what I want from now on. That's what I need."

"I'll try."

"I mean, you were so ardent in those letters."

He coiled a length of her hair around his finger. "Ardent, huh?"

"Hmm," she agreed. "Read some more to me."

"How about a new one?"

She nodded.

"I'll be right back."

Randy yanked on a robe and she heard him take the stairs to the garage. When he climbed back into bed a few minutes later, he said, "I'm freezing now. You're going to have to warm me up."

Facing him, she opened her arms. Her body felt so warm against him. But when his fingers touched her skin, she recoiled. "You *are* freezing!"

"Then, you have your work cut out for you." He chuckled, nuzzling her neck.

"Not until you read me that letter."

"Aw..." he groaned good-naturedly.

"C'mon," she said, getting comfortable again.

He had a feeling she purposely adjusted the blankets until they rested against her skin, draping elegantly over her curves in a way that accelerated Randy's thaw.

He faced her, lying on his side.

Jordan's hair spread beneath her head, falling over her shoulder and along her neck. Sleep lingered in her eyes, which she closed, preparing to listen.

He unfolded the pages and began.

Chapter Fifteen

My dear J,
I can't believe I'm here at the cabin and you're far away at home. How did we get to this place? What happened? It really hurts that you're not with me. But when I look around I know you never really liked it here.

Jordan opened her eyes. "That's because I didn't feel like I belonged with you there. You and the boys roughin' it, sure. But me? It's not that I'm above that; I just felt...left out."

Randy lowered the letter, searched her face. "I never said you didn't belong, did I?"

She shook her head.

"You were always welcome there. Aaron, Cass and I loved being there, sure. But it wouldn't have been the same without you. You belong wherever we are, honey."

She closed her eyes as he molded his hand against her face. "Maybe we can vacation there next summer. You can add whatever you like to the place; make it feel more like yours."

Jordan opened her eyes, seeking his face. "Really? You wouldn't feel I was desecrating the place?"

He chuckled. "Desecrating the place? It's not a shrine, Jae. It's a cabin."

"Okay. Let's plan it." She grinned. "That'd be fun."

He felt a full smile spread across his face. *Yes!* "Whew. I'm glad we finally talked that through. I never knew you didn't feel welcome. I wish you could have known Granddad. He'd have made you feel like a queen on a visit—more than welcome, appreciated, wanted. I'm sorry I didn't do that for you."

She ran a finger over a fold in the blankets. "It's like you get into your own world when we go there. The boys could bring you out of it a bit, but I just felt...like an extra."

A thought occurred to Randy. "How often do you feel that way? Unwanted, unwelcome, like an extra?"

"Not very." She ran her fingertip over his chest. "We've made this house a home for all four of us. It's only when I'm on your turf that I feel like a tag-along. Or when you have a deadline."

Randy winced. "I'm sorry. I know that was difficult, especially since both of us got sick." He leaned down and kissed her face, his eyes roving gently over her.

She noticed. "Better get back to the letter."

"I'm going to do better." He met her gaze. "I am."

She grinned. "I believe you. Please, read on."

She settled back then, closed her eyes and

waited.

Randy pushed up onto an elbow and continued.

You might accuse me of running away. You're probably right. I run here because I always have. When Granddad was alive, he always had wisdom and strategies that would help. This place is great for thinking through problems.

You wanna know why I've held myself back all these years? You know more about my father than anyone. I've told you about Dad's temper and his getting out of control. He wounded me. He destroyed my mother. Although I've prayed about it a million times, I still feel tempted to hate him. He's the reason I don't get worked up and I'm glad. I have never wanted to hurt you like he hurt me. I thought by keeping my own temper in check, I was protecting you. (Of course the differences between Dad and I make for a long list, starting with my redemption and Dad's rebellion.) Yeah, I thought I was doing the right thing. But I wonder about that now.

Does corralling all possible anger mean I'm also halting passion? Does limiting anger mean I can't feel other powerful emotions? Joy? That I'm missing out on life? Hmm. I believe God will heal me, forgive me and make me free. I trust Him to take that burden of anger against my father away from me. I trust Him to tame me, to be my guard, to be my Father.

I am so thankful that while He is doing that,

I get to love you.

So, I'm going to come home. Maybe if I show you all the letters, you'll believe what I've always felt in my heart to be true. Sorry I haven't been able to communicate it very well and that I've been locked up all this time.

Randy reached for the tendril of hair that was slipping over her neck and down her front. He wrapped it around his fingers. "You are where my heart is."

Sleepily, she offered, "Hmm..."

Randy picked up with that line:

You're where my heart is. I know God will show me how to make sure you know I love you beyond a shadow of a doubt. Granddad told me something once. He said, "When you find the woman you are going to commit your life to, don't forget, you're committing every part of yourself to her. Give yourself to her. She'll give herself back." That's what I want, J. I want to give myself to you. I've held back. It's true. You've held back, too, huh?

Oh, J. So, we're not perfect. Big surprise. But I want another chance. Another opportunity to prove I'm strong enough to do this—to give all of me to you. I know God reserves what is His. But I think we have more to give each other than we've even touched before now. I think that's part of the point. Trusting, giving, risking and living. Yeah. And loving.

I want to touch you. I want to hear you breathing, inhale your fragrance and taste your skin. Oh, J. I wish you were here right now.

So, I'll bring in the letters I did write. I'll risk your reaction because taking no risks in our relationship is getting us nowhere. Actually, it's what got me here. Alone.

I'm coming home, J. Get ready, honey, because I won't be denied. And, guess what? Neither will you.

With all my heart, Randy

Randy let the letter drop to the floor beside the bed. He leaned over and kissed Jordan right above where the sheet ended. When he pulled back, he saw tears running into her pillowcase.

"Jae?" He stroked her face. "Honey?"

She opened her eyes. "I've been withholding my heart, too." She sniffed. "I've been afraid you'd reject me. Actually, I wondered if you had rejected me a long time ago."

He winced and caressed her shoulder. "I could never do that. You're part of me, honey."

"I know I haven't been very open with you, either. I want to take more risks."

Randy smiled. "Me, too. Let's keep working on us. What do you say?"

She looked up at him, tears glistening in her eyes. "Love me?"

"With all my heart," he answered and slipped closer until the warmth he had stirred in each of them mixed. "With all my heart."

A word about the author...

Annette M. Irby enjoys writing songs, articles and novels. Her work has appeared in Northwest Christian Author, The Christian Journal, the devotional The Secret Place, and the 365-day devotional book Penned from the Heart, vols. xii and xiii (SonRise Publications, 2006 and 2007). Her current fiction writing includes a trilogy of novels, as well as novellas. She is a member of American Christian Fiction Writers and the Northwest Christian Writer's Association. She was a finalist in ACFW's Genesis Contest, 2006. Married 15 years, she lives with her husband and three children near Seattle, Washington.

Visit Annette at www.annetteirby.com